Max half hoped she'd tell him to give up, that she wanted him for herself.

Face it, genius. You wouldn't turn her down even if you're not on the same page. Not even the same book.

They could only be together if this was Ava's idea. If she could meet him halfway. Because if she didn't want him to find someone else, she might be forced to explore why. Whether that was good or bad for him, the sooner he knew, the sooner he could get Ava off his mind and move on.

Especially after that kiss.

"I just...don't know what you want, other than personality, and a good résumé."

"What if I make you a list?"

She crossed her arms. "A list?"

"A list of what I'm looking for in a woman."

"I'm beginning to regret that kiss. If you have double Ds on your list, I'm going to light it on fire."

"Ha. That's how little you know me." He tipped back on his heels. "I'm an ass-and-legs man."

She went palms up. "Give me your stupid list, and if I'm still talking to you after I read it, I'll see what I can do."

Dear Reader,

Welcome to the second book in the Charming, Texas miniseries! I hope you love *The Charming Checklist* as much as I do. Max and Ava were characters that were begging me to tell their story. And I do love a Grumpy vs. Sunshine trope. From the first time he walked onto the page, I pictured Max very clearly in my mind. He was a Latin James Bond, exquisitely dressed, could kill you with one finger. Max is a former navy SEAL who has worked hard to get to where he is now—a successful businessman. Having accomplished so many of his goals and dreams, Max mistakenly thinks he can find a wife by working just as hard at the task.

Ava is everybody's cheerleader, and she quite naturally gravitates to helping Max with his pursuit. That's where the checklist comes in. I don't want to ruin anything for you, but watch what happens when an overachiever thinks he can also "achieve" love and marriage. Of course, as happens so many times, the perfect woman is right under his nose, so to speak. She's the very woman he's asked to find him the perfect wife. And even she doesn't realize how perfect they are together!

I do hope that you enjoy this friends-to-lovers, Grumpy vs. Sunshine romance!

Drop me a line anytime, as I love to hear from you, at heatherly@heatherlybell.com.

Happy reading!

Heatherly

The Charming Checklist

HEATHERLY BELL

HARLEQUIN

SPECIAL
EDITION

ISBN-13: 978-1-335-40830-3

The Charming Checklist

Copyright © 2021 by Heatherly Bell

This edition published by arrangement with Harlequin Books S.A.

For questions and comments about the quality of this book,
please contact us at CustomerService@Harlequin.com.

Harlequin Enterprises ULC
22 Adelaide St. West, 41st Floor
Toronto, Ontario M5H 4E3, Canada
www.Harlequin.com

Printed in U.S.A.

Heatherly Bell tackled her first book in 2004, and now the characters that occupy her mind refuse to leave until she writes them a book. She loves all music but confines singing to the shower these days. Heatherly lives in Northern California with her family, including two beagles—one who can say hello and the other a princess who can feel a pea through several pillows.

Books by Heatherly Bell

Harlequin Special Edition

Charming, Texas

Winning Mr. Charming

Wildfire Ridge

More than One Night
Reluctant Hometown Hero
The Right Moment

Harlequin Superromance

Heroes of Fortune Valley

Breaking Emily's Rules
Airman to the Rescue
This Baby Business

Visit the Author Profile page
at Harlequin.com for more titles.

For Shadow, Kiara, Riley and Jack,
our loyal and loving family pets

Chapter One

Tonight seemed like the perfect night for Max Del Toro to find a wife.

On Friday, the Salty Dog Bar & Grill in Charming, Texas, was fairly empty, not unusual for mid-October on the Gulf Coast. Most of the summer tourists were gone and only the locals were left. He took a seat on an empty bar stool and simply nodded in Cole Kinsella's direction, holding up his index finger.

Within seconds Cole plunked his usual IPA in front of him. "You're a little dressed up. You have that date tonight, right?"

Cole, his best friend and business partner at the Salty Dog, was more curious than most about his personal life. Max didn't mind. They went far back, to their days as part of an elite SEALs team.

Max took a pull of his beer. He happened to be wearing his best suit, and a lot of faith. "With any luck, I might find the future Mrs. DT tonight."

"Don't get your hopes up." Cole gave the bar a wipe.

Coming from a man who'd recently been reunited with his first love, that seemed ironic. Max had given Cole and Valerie Villanueva long odds, and yet they were now planning a spring wedding. Max figured Cole beat the odds, so why couldn't he?

"Seems shortsighted of you," Max said.

"Why? I never had the best luck with blind dates. Who has? I mean, c'mon!"

That might be true if Max hadn't done the leg-work. This wasn't technically a blind date. He'd put in the hard nights, filling out those ridiculous online questionnaires. Favorite color, music, food, wine. Beach or woods? Ocean or lake? Exhausting work, all of it. He'd rather climb Mount Kilimanjaro or swim to Galveston. He didn't see what his favorite *color* had to do with anything, but he'd put his trust in these services. One of them reported a 99.9 percent rate of success. Those were damn good odds.

"Not a blind date. I've done my homework."

Max would approach finding the perfect wife in the same way that he did anything in his life. With a plan, a road map and high odds for success. For a kid who'd come from the strawberry-picking fields

of Watsonville, California, to become a savvy businessman, planning was *everything*. At thirty-four,
it was time to settle down and find a wife. He'd approach this goal the same way he'd achieved all of his
success: by doing more than expected of him. He'd
signed up for every single one of these services and
had dates lined up for six months. But it shouldn't
take *that* long to find the right woman.

"You haven't heard any of the horror stories?"

"Of course I have. Probably from people who
didn't approach this as analytically as I have."

"That's one way of lookin' at it," Cole muttered.

The door opened and Max turned to see Ava
Long, president of the Chamber of Commerce, make
her way to the bar. Blonde and beautiful, she had an
ass that should be declared the eighth wonder of the
world. Again, as he did nearly every day of the week,
Max pushed aside the attraction. They were friends
and it would be best not to mess with that, tempting
though she was.

"Hi, Cole! Oh, hey there, Max," she added almost as an afterthought. "Hey, is Valerie working
tonight?"

As always, she had the enthusiasm of Christmas Day. Bright. Merry. A friend to everyone. She
hugged Valerie every time she saw her, which was
just about daily. As usual, she wore every color under
the rainbow. Why not, when one of them might get
their feelings hurt. Pink, purple and green top. Blue

slacks with white stripes. Black-and-white-checkered high tops.

The rest of Ava, her personality, was a little hard for Max to take in anything but small doses.

"Nah, gave her the night off. She's at home with Sub," Cole said.

Submarine, known as Sub, was Cole's loyal Labrador retriever. He'd become the bar's mascot and usually lounged in the back office whenever both Cole and Valerie pulled a shift.

"I have a little announcement to make," Ava said.

"Go ahead." Cole waved in the direction of their customers.

She moved to the middle of the room that divided the bar from the small open dining area.

"Attention, everyone!" She clapped her hands, waved and waited for everyone to hush. "As you all know, the holiday food drive is in full swing! The Chamber is spearheading the event again and we've got barrels all over the city. Let's fill them up this year so that they're overflowing this holiday! The low-income families and the needy in Charming will thank you. Nonperishables only!"

How about that, she even made being low income and needy sound joyful. Max remembered being on the other side of that coin. Hiding behind his parents as they accepted all the well-meant charity from strangers. He'd come a long way from those less-than-pleasant memories, from those times when he'd been the charity case that wore hand-me-downs.

Well, he wasn't going to think about that now.

When she rejoined them, Max reached for his wallet, and pulled out two hundred-dollar bills and handed them to her. "I don't have any canned food in the house."

"Thank you, Max," she said, staring at the bills. "You're more than generous."

"You're welcome." He shrugged. "Figured you could do the shopping."

"I love shopping!"

Again, with all the enthusiasm. The joy. She might not realize that some of the people on the receiving end of charity didn't find their situation particularly joyous. He understood this better than most.

Max stood, not finishing the rest of his drink. "I'm out of here."

He'd made reservations for his date with Grace Fitzpatrick at Le Oranguan, the expensive and swanky restaurant on the rooftop of The Lookout, the only hotel in Charming. He'd come prepared for a G-rated evening with a woman he wanted to get to know better. If Max wanted sex, he could find that easily enough. But for the past year, he'd been in training to be someone's husband. Therefore, he'd deprived himself of the casual companionship of women. It was time to get serious. Go deep.

At least on paper, he and Grace were a perfect match. She was a graduate of Columbia University in New York, summa cum laude, currently in Texas working on her doctorate in mathematics. Thirty-two, and never married, she enjoyed cooking, her favorite color was blue and she wanted four children. Max preferred the color black, he enjoyed eating more so than cooking, but he also wanted four children. He wanted each of those four children to have the best start in life, with two educated and highly professional parents who could give them the best of everything.

Max had taken care of his half. He was educated, successful and a long way from the picking fields of Watsonville. The fact that some women found him good-looking, but a little emotionally stunted, was of no concern to him now. He'd work on that, since he had literally everything else to offer a woman.

Tonight he expected an evening full of stimulating topics and discussion. He wanted an interesting and sophisticated woman who would challenge him intellectually. The picture Grace posted was a flattering one but looks weren't as important long-term. She hit every one of his requirements out of the ballpark when it came to background and education. Now he needed to learn more about her personality. Her beauty should be more than skin-deep.

Oh, he wasn't a snob, not him, but he simply didn't want his children to work as hard as he had. And if he were going to eventually grow the Salty Dog Bar & Grill into a chain restaurant, as he hoped, it would be nice to have a wife who would be comfortable in high society and throwing a first-class dinner party for his colleagues by having all the right contacts.

He'd determined not to get deeply involved or connected to anyone until everything else was lined up perfectly. Until he found someone who he could spend the rest of his life with. He could not and would not be derailed from his goal. Max arrived early so he could scope out the area and make sure their table location was perfect. He also preferred to sit with no one to his back, but that was a holdover from his navy SEAL days, and his only real quirk.

"Right this way Mr. Del Toro," the maître d' said, and then waving to the table, "Is everything to your satisfaction?"

He gave the table a quick perusal and glanced at his nautical wristwatch. "Yes, perfect, thank you. My date will be arriving shortly."

"I'll send her right over."

This shouldn't take long. Max figured if the first date was a good connection, as he hoped, they wouldn't have to linger over dinner. No need to be tempted to get physical too fast if there was a serious attraction. He'd just schedule another date, this time on the beach, so he could see how she handled a little sand and surf.

Grace waltzed in right on time, as beautiful as her photo, and he unkinked his shoulders. Cole made Max think that maybe someone else might show up. But this was the same woman in the photo. Tall, brunette, slender. They would make beautiful children.

He rose to greet her and offered his hand. "I'm Max."

"You're just like your photo!" She went hand to

chest and gently sat when he pulled out her chair. "You have no idea how many of these dates I've been on, and *no* one looks like their photo."

"That's a shame. Why would anyone waste their time like that? It's completely illogical." He sat and snapped his menu shut. "Should we order?"

"Nothing for me," she said. "I don't eat."

"You don't eat."

Now, that was a lie. If she didn't eat, she'd be dead by now. Max supposed that was a ridiculous way to avoid chewing in front of him and she lost points for that.

"Not after six," she added.

"I'm sorry, you should have said something."

"Well, you know what? I'll have a green salad."

Max ordered for both of them and was pleasantly surprised at the flow of conversation. He asked questions about her work and she answered them without hesitation. Best of all, the entire time she remained cool and collected. Smooth. Her personality and temperament were even and subdued. Hard to rattle her, he had to assume. Very nice. He could listen to her talk for hours, which he realized he would have to do if they were eventually married. Yeah. This could work.

She reached for his hand. "Max, you don't talk much, but I think this is going well. Do you agree?"

"I agree. We should schedule another time to meet."

As an added bonus, he didn't find himself having to restrain any physical impulses with this woman.

This would make it easier to get to know each other. Of course, if the physical attraction didn't work itself out later, that could be a problem. But he refused to think about that now. There was no reason he shouldn't be attracted to Grace, who was a beautiful woman.

"Would you excuse me a minute?"

She was gone longer than Max would have thought likely for the restroom, and he began to wonder if she'd walked out on him. It would be the first time it had ever happened to him. Usually he walked out first, when emotions got too heated and complicated. But even if it had been over a decade since he'd felt the shame of not being good enough, a sliver of alarm rolled through him. This was not what he'd signed up for.

When she came back, she seemed a little flushed. "I never do this."

"You never do what?"

"Take a chance like this one." She removed a room key from her purse and didn't meet his eyes. "I got us a room for the night. Max, you're the sexiest man I've ever met."

He blinked. Of all the things he expected, this was the last. "Uh, thanks—"

"I hope I'm not being too aggressive, but a woman in my profession just doesn't meet men who look like you. And I'm a modern woman with *needs*. Know what I mean? What do you say?"

Damn. Something a little like relief rolled through

him, like the time he thought he'd blown the officer's exam, only to find he'd had the highest score in years. But this was certainly an unexpected turn of events. He really liked Grace, but he wanted to check out who else might be out there, and it seemed unfair to sleep with her and then move on. That's not what this was about. From now on, he would save himself for his future wife.

When he didn't respond for several seconds, she licked her lips and palmed his thigh. "I hope I haven't ruined things between us now."

And then the scariest thought of all suddenly hit Max: he did not *want* to sleep with this woman! This didn't make sense, as she was beautiful, not crazy, and he should at least be *tempted*. He was tempted every time he saw Ava, after all, and she was wrong for him on every level.

"Not at all," Max lied. "But I have other plans tonight. I'll call you."

Chapter Two

Ava Long sat at the bar sipping her Coffee Keoke and avoiding thoughts of her birthday next week. Her entire family would be making their annual trek from Dallas to Charming to check on her plans for world domination. Both of her parents, Dr. and Dr. Long, and her brothers, Dr. Long and Dr. Long. Not that *she* called them that, just everyone else did. It became confusing at times.

Yes, I'm Dr. Long and I'm here to meet Dr. Long and Dr. Long. We have reserved a table for five.

A birthday should be a time of celebration, but for her it was a time of explanation. She was beginning to resent it. They couldn't seem to accept that she was happy and satisfied with her life. She lived

in Charming, a small bucolic town on the Gulf Coast
with beautiful beaches, a nonworking lighthouse and
quaint cottages. Her job single-handedly running
the Chamber of Commerce meant that she met a lot
of the residents and business owners. She thrived
in her position, helping others, coordinating events
and parties for the business community. Occasionally working closely with the mayor, Tippi Goodwill.

Of course, she hadn't made much progress on her
actual dream, but her family was even less excited
about that.

"Another coffee?" Cole asked.

"No, I'm okay."

"Hey, did you notice Max was wearing a suit?"
Cole polished a glass.

Oh boy, had she. Hard not to. Max in a suit was
like a Latin James Bond. Tall. Dark. Shaken, not
stirred. Could kill you with one finger.

"He's dating."

"Really? *Max?*"

She figured that Max would never *date*. He'd just
go up to a woman, entice her and take her back to
his place. She'd come along willingly because, seriously, *Max Del Toro*. End of story. Though he probably wouldn't be a good date because he was grumpy
all the time and talked very little. Even less to Ava.
She usually did all the talking around him. Tonight,
she'd gotten more than two words out of him but
that was rare.

"Yeah, he signed up with the online dating services."

Why on earth Max would sign up for a dating service? Even tonight, the beautiful and very available Twyla couldn't take her eyes off him.

"Which one?"

"All of them."

"*All* of them?"

"Max's an overachiever. He's the guy you always wanted to have your back. Pretty sure he thinks he can find the perfect wife just by working hard at the task."

"A wife? He wants to get *married*?"

"That's what he says. Says its time. I tried to tell him love doesn't work that way, but he wouldn't listen. He puts a lot of faith in logic, but love isn't logical half the time. Is it?"

"I guess not."

Her family, of course, would say otherwise. Besides conquering her little slice of pie in the world, they expected her to marry an educated and highly successful man.

Ava's phone rang in her purse. The theme from *Jaws*, so this would be Mom calling, Dr. Katherine Long.

"I better take this." She pulled out her phone. "Hi, Mom."

"Your father made reservations at Le Oranguan for Saturday night, six o'clock."

As usual her parents were going to splurge on dinner. That rooftop restaurant was the most expensive in town. It wasn't so much Ava her parents were trying to impress as complete strangers. They'd order the most expensive bottle of champagne and begin toasting the year's accomplishments thus far.

"That's an expensive restaurant."

"Only the best for my only daughter."

"But, Mom, I'm—"

"Stop. It's decided, and must you argue with me about everything?"

"I don't argue about everything!" And yes, she realized the irony of arguing over this.

"Any more thoughts on taking the LSAT? You'd ace the test *and* law school. Lots of great chances to use those amazing argumentative skills."

"I told you, Mom. I *want* to be an entrepreneur."

"Please don't tell me you're still stuck on that coffee shop idea."

"It's not an idea. It's a plan."

"It's as if you don't even remember that your father is a cardiac surgeon. Coffee puts your heart in a race it can't win."

"But all the latest studies show that moderation is the key."

"Do you have an answer for everything?"

"Yes."

"And that's precisely why you'd do so well in law school. You do your research. We all know you're smart and capable. Why would you want to open up a *coffee shop*?"

"I've got to go. I'm getting to that part of town where reception is kind of…spo…ty… I…talk…ter." Ava pressed end call.

"Still telling her there's spotty reception in Charming, huh?" Cole smiled.

"Don't judge."

Cole held up his palms but when the door opened, his eyes gravitated in that direction, and Ava's gaze naturally followed. Max stalked toward the bar.

"He looks pissed. I bet it didn't go well," Cole said.

"Uh-oh. She probably put up a fake photo and didn't even look like herself. I've heard women do that. Men, too."

"You should probably go. There's going to be some angry guy talk going on."

"I'm sorry, but you couldn't pay me to leave now. This should be good."

Max straddled the stool next to Ava and unloosened his tie, twisting it as though it ticked him off simply by daring to hang around his neck. "Not talking."

Cole set an IPA down. "That bad, huh?"

"Was she a lot older than her picture? Fifty pounds heavier? Not a woman?" Ava said.

Max closed his eyes and pinched the bridge of his nose. "No. Just like her picture."

"I *saw* her picture," Cole said. "That woman was beautiful. Almost as beautiful as Valerie, which is a pretty high bar for me."

"Did she talk all night about an ex?" Ava asked. Max shook his head.

"Let me ask you this." Max turned to Ava, hands resting on the lapels of his suit. "Do you like this suit? Does it look cheap?"

Ava swallowed. "Not at all. You look cool and sophisticated. As if you should be asking for your martini shaken, not stirred."

"What's this about?" Cole asked.

"This is another question for Ava." Max ignored Cole. "Do I look like someone on the prowl?"

"Wh-what?" Ava stammered.

"As if I'm looking to get laid." Max nearly spit the words out.

"I'm, uh…uh…you…um…" It was as if she'd forgotten the English language.

"I don't think I've ever seen Ava tongue-tied." Cole grinned, apparently enjoying this far too much.

"Never mind." Max turned back to Cole. "My future prospective wife got us a hotel room for the night within thirty minutes of meeting me."

"What are you doing *here*?" Cole gaped.

"I'm serious about this. No more fooling around. I'm going to get to know a woman and see how compatible we are before I sleep with her."

Cole bent over with laughter and excused himself, going to the other end of the bar before Max killed him with that little finger of his, Ava assumed. She was also having a difficult time smothering a laugh, but there was another side of her that was intrigued. And also, a little afraid of the finger thing.

"You signed up for *all* the dating services?"

"That's right. I have dates lined up for months but after tonight, I'm discouraged. Maybe I should take my photo out and see how many takers I get."

It was as if she'd just dropped into an alternate universe. He was *serious.*

"That's one thing you could do."

"I'm looking for someone who's interested in my résumé, not how much I can bench-press."

She snorted. "Of course. At this time, I really should apologize for women everywhere. We're not all interested in treating a man like a piece of meat."

Again, had she fallen through the looking glass?

"Maybe I should look up your profile and give you some advice."

Watching Max navigate this new world of his was like a traffic accident. Or a bad reality show. Trash TV, Valerie called it. And they both indulged one night a week, the fiancé show their current binge. It was awesome.

"I mean, you could always use a woman's touch, right?"

Max quirked a brow and nodded. "All right, Miss Congeniality, tell me what you think."

He scrolled through his phone and handed it to Ava. The photo he'd chosen for his profile would make any woman drool. She'd bet half of his prospective dates didn't believe it was an honest photo.

It was a little too good to be true and she'd bet they showed up just to find out. She would.

"Hmm."

"What?"

His résumé, such as he'd described it, *was* impressive. In addition to all his military service in Special Forces, he'd worked as CEO for a high-tech company in Austin and started half a dozen businesses including the Salty Dog. He had an MBA in business, which surprised even her. All this and he was only thirty-four. And she thought she knew Max. Lord help her, like Cole, he'd been a former navy SEAL, but she'd had no idea he was also this educated and accomplished. Her family would adore him. He wasn't a doctor, sure, but one could almost call him a doctor in the field of business.

She scrolled through a few photos and found one of him holding a surfboard. The board hid most of his amazing physique, and the fading sun gave his face an almost average look.

"I'd make *this* your profile photo." She tapped the phone. "This way, the woman also knows that you can look and do casual. And that you love the water."

"Good idea." He took his phone back with a look of surprise.

"Well, don't give me that look. I give *fantastic* advice."

"Yeah? How much do you know about these dating services?"

"Nothing. *I'd* never do it."

"Why not?"

"Love doesn't work that way!"

He chuckled. "What way? Do you mean two people finding whether or not they're compatible and have similar goals choosing to date and see what materializes?"

"Well, sorry, but that sounds a little too logical for love. Love just *happens*, Max."

"To idiots."

"Are you calling Valerie and Cole idiots? Because I swear, I'm telling."

"Love doesn't just happen." One side of Max's mouth curled in a smirk. "They beat the odds."

And maybe Ava could, too. Maybe this birthday dinner wouldn't be about explaining how she'd once again failed to start her own business and become the next Martha Stewart of the coffee bean world. At least she could demonstrate that she was associating with the right people.

Ava studied Max as he scrolled through his phone and finished his IPA. If she took him to her birthday dinner as her date, dressed in this suit, and her family saw *his* résumé, they'd be suitably impressed. He was one of them. She would at least be dating someone who her family would approve of, even if they wouldn't approve of her.

"Um, Max?"

He gave her a sideways look as if surprised to still find her there. "Yeah."

"Would you like to go to dinner with me next Saturday night and meet my parents?"

He blinked. "Meeting the parents on a first date? No thanks. That's a little fast even for me, but hey, thanks for asking."

Ava laughed a bit maniacally. "Oh, ha! No. You misunderstood me. I meant come to dinner with me as a friend. But maybe… I don't know…pretend to be more than my friend? Just for one night."

"Pretend?" His brow furrowed giving him a highly concerned look.

He was probably wondering how fast he could get out of this without hurting a friend's feelings.

She waved her hands in front of her like a crazy woman. "Let me explain. My family is from Dallas, but they all come to Charming to take me out to dinner every year on my birthday."

"That's nice."

"Nice? No, not *nice*. It's an inspection. They're going to analyze my life. Suggest what career might be best for me."

"But you already have a career."

"Do you think that matters to them? It's not good enough for Dr. Long, Dr. Long, and don't forget Dr. Long and Dr. Long."

He squinted. "You're repeating yourself."

"No, those are my parents and my two brothers. All medical doctors who excel in their fields. My brothers are married with Stepford wives. Cocktail parties, one-thousand-dollar-a-plate fundraisers, perfectly behaved genius children, you name it. My family are a bunch of snobs."

"And what happened to *you*?" he deadpanned.

She wasn't at all offended. In fact, it always instilled a sense of pride in her when anyone asked.

"Right? I'm the furthest thing from a snob. I love this quaint little town and our small business community. Someday, I want to start my own business. But I digress. My family would be extremely impressed with you. I mean, I just read your résumé."

"Exactly! And you probably weren't thinking about sleeping with me after you did."

"Absolutely not." *Before, yes. Now, not so much.* "I'm all about that incredible résumé."

"I'm flattered."

"So, what do you say, pal?" She elbowed him. "It would be more date practice for you, after all."

He pulled out his wallet from his inside pocket and slid a few bills on the bar. That single move was solidly sexy, not to mention the move of a man used to paying. A man used to moving through important circles with confidence. Her excitement rose as it did when she'd roasted a particular good batch of coffee beans.

This charade could work.

"They'll see right through me if they're as intelligent as you've described. I have to say no. But thanks. You've given me hope."

He patted her hand, flashed her a rare smile and then he was gone.

Chapter Three

The next morning, Ava blinked her eyes open and stretched. The morning sunrays gleamed through her blue lace curtains and a warm, salty ocean breeze wafted through the window she'd left cracked open. She was in her cozy bed in her tiny cottage on Monroe Street, about half a mile from the beach. As the cobwebs began to unfurl in her mind, a trickle of a memory rose to the forefront.

Last night was a complete bust.

What did it say about her that she couldn't even get a *fake* date with someone like Max Del Toro?

Maybe it says that you're not ready for permanent, and you've just asked a man who's on the hunt for permanent to join you on a fake date.

With your entire family.

Oh, yeah. She rubbed her eyes. But hey, it had been worth a try. If he wanted to go on more of those service-arranged dates, he was welcome to it. She, however, could probably find the perfect wooden woman for him without even trying. After all, she'd grown up and gone to school with women like her sisters-in-law. Clearly, Max was more like her family than she'd realized. He wanted a Stepford wife. A trophy wife.

Or maybe it was just easier to think that than to believe he'd turned her down based on her looks. Or worse, her *personality.* A little too much wattage to handle all at once. Like she hadn't heard that one before. Every other day someone told her to "tone it down." Reminded her that it wasn't Christmas yet, just another annual Charming town event. Like the Mr. Charming contest, which she'd made into their most successful to date. She couldn't help that life and new adventures thrilled her and she couldn't contain her joy at meeting new people and learning new things. These qualities would all come together for her on the day she finally opened up her coffee shop.

The Bean.

Little Beans.

The Magic Bean.

Well, she was still experimenting with names.

Like Max, her family, and everyone who knew her family, wondered where and how everything went wrong with her. The explanation was quite simple.

She was the only daughter and youngest child of three. With two always working professionals for parents, she'd been raised by her nanny. A woman she'd loved like a grandmother. But Lucia Perez had moved back to Colombia when Ava went away to college. She'd received a generous severance and bonus package from her parents for her years of dedicated service. Last Ava had heard Lucia had purchased a home. Ava regularly got a Christmas card and a birthday card from Nanny Lucia. Funny, she never once asked if Ava had achieved an executive-level position yet, or finally decided to go to law or medical school.

Instead, she'd send her a new recipe for roasting beans. New combinations of flavors. She'd ask about her friends, her job, her love life. Remind her that she was loved and perfect just as she was. And Nanny Lucia was the only person who still wrote letters to Ava. She didn't have or believe in cell phones. Texting thoroughly confused her.

Because of her, Ava still associated the smell and taste of a good cup of coffee with love. With warmth and acceptance. They used to spend hours roasting beans for the family. Ava hadn't been allowed to drink her first cup, of course, until she was fourteen. Then, a long love affair began.

Ava rolled out of bed, the beans calling her name. It was always best not to formulate full thoughts, not to mention sentences, before her first cup. Today was one of her favorite days of the week. Roasting beans day. She had a new bag of green coffee beans from a Colombian farmer through Lucia's connections. But for now, she pulled out her sealed roasted coffee bean bag and took out her grinder. Making a batch small enough for two, she then took out her French press. There was no point in going through all this trouble to put her beans through a *percolator*.

Quickly showering, then throwing on a T-shirt and jeans, she crossed the shared lawn to her favorite neighbor Susannah's home. From inside, she could hear her cockapoo mix, Doodle, giving his best impression of a menacing home protector. *Yip, yip, yip.* Yeah, not even close.

The minute the door opened and Ava walked inside, Doodle predictably rolled over on his back.

Ava handed the French press to Susannah and bent to pet Doodle. "Who's a good boy? Huh? Who's a good boy?"

"Smells divine," Susannah said, leading the way into the kitchen. "No one makes coffee like you do."

"That's what I'm hoping."

Ava helped Susannah with cups and saucers. Susannah took her coffee with a little milk and sugar because nobody was perfect. Ava preferred hers black so that she could experience every bold and rich texture and flavor. Susannah set down a Danish kringle, and they began their Saturday ritual. Coffee, sweets and gossip. Susannah was a contributing member of the Almost Dead Poet Society senior citizen's group and made it her business to keep up on all the latest Charming news through those connections. She kept inviting Ava to attend one of their meetings but so far Ava hadn't been able to make it.

"So...the official news is that Valerie and Cole nixed having their wedding as a Mr. and Mrs. Charming town event. Sorry, sugar. It appears to be their final answer."

"I know."

Ava didn't want to break it to Susannah, but being Valerie's best friend had perks, and she'd had that news for a while. "And they're entitled to make their wedding private and intimate."

"I didn't think you'd take this so well." Susannah patted Ava's hand. "I know how much you'd hoped to make this wedding pretty much a town-sponsored event."

"Well, it would have been nice, but I understand Valerie's position." She took her first sip of coffee and nearly had a religious experience. "Oh, this batch came out amazing."

"They all do." She stirred sugar in her coffee cup, leaned forward and smiled. "And also, Max Del Toro is dating!"

Ava didn't have the heart to pretend she didn't also already have this gossip. "Oh. Really."

"Valerie told us at the last poetry meeting. Imagine this—he's signed up for all the dating services. One does question the wisdom of this decision."

One does. "Well, he's joining millions of single people who can't all be wrong."

Susannah cut through the Danish and served Ava. "In my day, we went to the sock hop and the roller-skating rink."

"Well, I don't think this is going to work, and then Max will probably just give up. Unless he lets me fix him up."

"You could find someone for him?"

"I probably could throw a rock in my senior graduating class and find him the perfect woman."

"Why not you, sugar?" Susannah winked.

"Other than the fact that Max scares me a little bit? He wants to get married. I'm definitely not interested in marriage."

She'd made a choice to be more like Nanny Lucia.

There's a time for everything and now is the time to raise children and roast coffee beans, she'd said in her accented English. *When I was a younger woman I used to dance on tabletops and drink tequila. And date handsome men.*

Ava would be twenty-nine next week, still relatively young, so she'd be a career woman until it was time to marry and have children. After that, she'd put all her focus on raising her children. She did want children. One or two, tops. No need to get crazy. But like everything else she did in life, Ava would do it with gusto. Her children would finger paint and mold with clay. They'd go to the park and swing until they were dizzy. She wouldn't insist on color-coordinated outfits. They could dress themselves in unmatching outfits. She wouldn't sign them up for SAT prep courses in fifth grade. In fact, she wouldn't even in-sist on college—gasp!—unless they wanted to go.

After coffee, Ava went home to get ready for her plans today. Although this was part of her position as the president—and full staff—of the Chamber of Commerce, Ava would have done it anyway. Today, the ribbon-cutting ceremony for the grand opening of Hot Threads, a yarn specialty store on Main Street, would take place. She'd be in attendance with her trusty phone camera, ready to take photos, upload them and splash them all over the town's website to get the word out for a new business owner in town. Community support was vital to success.

Someday, that would be her.

Max spent the first part of his Saturday on the water. He kayaked in the early morning before the sun rose. Cole had failed to join him on the waves this morning—something about picking out a wed-ding cake. He did, however, drop off Sub so that at least he could have a go at the waves.

Sub ran and chased at the edge of the surf while Max kayaked several feet out, keeping a close watch on him. Not that he had to. Sub was as loyal as they came, the best kind of dog. Later, he took Sub back to his condo near the beach where they would watch football and wait for Cole.

Max set a bowl of water down. "Have at it."

Sub slurped and splashed all over the wood floor, then lay on the floor like a rug.

Max dried up the water Sub had spilled, then showered and shaved. He considered what he should wear tonight for his date with Daphne Montgomery. Ava would probably tell him to come in his board shorts and a tee. He spent enough time on the water to consider it. But Max figured a graduate of MIT, and a woman registered with the MENSA society, would much prefer the suit. Surely Daphne would not get them a hotel room for the night. Just to be safe he'd made reservations at the Crow's Nest. No hotel attached or even nearby.

It wasn't that he didn't love sex because he did. Maybe a little *too* much. The words *sex addict* had been bandied about by a few ex-girlfriends. Completely untrue. He'd never cheated, and Max didn't believe in so-called sex addiction. He figured that was just another label invented by men to excuse their bad behavior. Another term for "playboy" or "commitment-phobe." That certainly had never been him, much as he'd enjoyed sex. It just had always seemed that there could be someone better out there and he hadn't been ready to settle down.

But he worried his sometimes-roving eye could be the reason he'd been fantasizing about Ava lately. Her shapely behind, legs, long, kissable neck and sensual mouth said fun with a capital *F*. Which went right along with his favorite *F* word. But his life would have to change. Having amazing sex was not known to be the best way to find a compatible partner for the long haul. A real damn shame, but he'd done the research. The facts didn't lie.

Cole arrived a few hours later to pick up Sub and accepted a cold beer.

"How'd it go?" Max asked.

"We went with whatever Valerie wanted because I can't distinguish between cake properties like I can with beer."

"Which is why we own a bar." Max clinked bottles with Cole.

"Amen, buddy. Amen." Cole bent to pet Sub, who had found a place on the floor on his feet. Not by them. *On* them. "I heard Ava asked you out."

"To impress her family."

The fact that Ava Long had asked him out to impress *her* family had been the most gratifying thing she'd said to him since the day he met her.

Years ago, the daughter of doctors would not have even been in Max's social circle, much less a friend.

"Ah, she must have that family birthday dinner again."

"Yep. I had no idea she had a family full of doctors. Must be interesting dinner conversation."

"Valerie says they're not very supportive of Ava and this dinner is just a way to criticize her in person instead of over the phone."

"On her birthday? Who would be that cruel?"

Cole shrugged. "Who's your date tonight?"

"Daphne Montgomery." Even her name slid off

his tongue smoothly. Max listed her achievements and background and watched as Cole's eyes widened.

"Man. Hope you can curl up to her big brain every night."

Smug, Cole went to his phone and brought up her photo. "I think there's far more than her brain I could be sleeping with."

"Oh, yeah. Wow. Why are all these women signing up for dating services? It sounds a little... I don't know, desperate? And, bro, she doesn't look desperate."

Admittedly, Max had his doubts about online dating profiles. He should have probably gone with an old-fashioned matchmaker and if this didn't work out, that would be his next move.

"Maybe like me they're looking for someone compatible. Or maybe they don't have time to filter through all the men knocking their doors down."

"Far be it from me to say, but not having enough time doesn't bode well for a serious relationship."

He'd cross that bridge when he came to it. At this point, he didn't expect to find the right woman for him immediately. It just didn't make sense and couldn't be that easy. Nothing worthwhile ever was.

Max had now indulged in enough small talk. He had to get to the point and knew Cole wouldn't like it. But he tended to be everybody's best friend and left the tough decisions to Max.

Like when to fire someone.

"We have to let him go, Cole."

"Not this again. I thought we were going to give Nick another chance."

"I don't give *anyone* a third chance."

"Because you're a hard-ass."

"That's why you love me. You're too damn nice, which is how you won Mr. Charming. But it's not how we're going to stay successful and grow. We need everyone to be on board. He's a link in the unbreakable chain and I want to cut him loose."

Nick, their chef, had been with the bar since long before their grand reopening a year ago. He'd worked for the previous owner. A great cook, but Max was sick of Nick's womanizing. He went home with a different woman every other night, which wasn't any of their business. But he was often late, or MIA after a random hookup, which was very much their business. Cole often took care of receiving the fish order on the days when it arrived because Nick was rarely there on time. Cole, of course, didn't mind. Max did.

And then there was the night three weeks ago when a jealous husband had come looking for Nick. Max covered for him, *once*, and he wouldn't be doing that again.

"Whatever you think." Cole didn't defend Nick, which meant he'd finally come to his senses. "You know I'm behind you."

Cole was that team member that refused to leave anyone behind. No matter what. But they weren't in the SEALs anymore where that was expected of them. Max believed that every link in a chain had to be unbreakable. Solid. This was business and Max made decisions without sentiment. No room for warm and fuzzy.

"Let's bring Adam on."

Adam Cruz had been on the same SEAL team with them, their most decorated member. Honorable. Loyal. Above reproach, Max would still trust him with his life.

"Are you sure he's ready?" When Sub whined for a rub, Cole relented, and rubbed behind his ears.

"I know he's ready for a change."

"Give him a call."

"Already did," Max said. "Made him an offer."

"And he accepted?"

Max nodded. "I'll wait until he gets here before I cut Nick loose."

It wasn't as though Nick was a top-rated chef, for which they'd probably put up with a lot of bad behavior. Max still had the goal of getting one of those in, but for now, slinging burgers, fried fish and steaks was something even he could do. Though he sure wouldn't want to be forced to attempt it. Mixing drinks at the bar was one thing, cooking quite another. He appreciated high-quality food but had little clue how to make it.

With that high quality in mind, later that day, Max arrived early for his dinner date.

"She's already here," the maître d' said.

It was enough to have Max glance at this wristwatch, but no, still early. Something else they already had in common. He followed the server to the table he'd selected in the back. Max blinked because *this* couldn't be right. An elderly woman sat at the table. Knitting.

Max stopped. "Are you sure this is the right table?"

"Yes, sir. Party for two. Daphne Montgomery."

There had to be some mistake. Unless he was about to encounter his first horror story. If this blue-haired granny believed she'd get away with this she had to be mentally unhinged. She was at least four decades past her stated age. The photo must have been of a professional cover model.

"Hello," he said to the woman, who squinted over her bifocals when she looked up from her knitting. "I'm Max Del Toro."

"You're kidding." She gaped.

He took a seat. "Not what you expected?"

"Not at all." She dropped her knitting and held up her index finger. "But hang on. I'll be right with you."

She pulled out a phone from her huge tote bag, put it to her ear and waited, winking at Max. "Honey, this is Grandma. Pick up, please. Call me back, stat! You won't believe what just happened."

"What's going on, Daphne?" he asked, with far more patience than he actually had left.

"I have a confession to make."

"No kidding."

"I'm not Daphne. That's my granddaughter." She

went hand to heart. "I'm Betty. But everything I posted about my granddaughter is true. And that's her picture! She claims she's not interested in dating, so I volunteered to do all the sorting for her."

"The sorting. How kind of you."

"I thought so. But she's not too thrilled with it. Actually, I haven't been, either. So far, it's been a lot of men showing up who are twenty years older than they claimed."

How ironic.

"Maybe if she's interested in dating, she should be the one meeting people. Just a suggestion."

Her phone rang. "This is her now. Honey, get over to the Crow's Nest right now. I've got a live one!"

And Max indeed felt like a fish caught in a net, wriggling with all his might to get back into the water where he could breathe. He was going to have to lodge a complaint with this particular service. This kind of bait and switch was inexcusable. Completely unprofessional. Then again, he'd been warned about fake online dating profiles. He knew better, too.

Who's the desperate one now?

No time to get bogged down in emotions. This was the time to make decisions and take action.

"Betty, I'm going to go." He stood. "Lovely meeting you. Say hi to your granddaughter."

"Hurry, hurry, he's leaving!" Betty screeched into the phone.

Max walked outside into the cool evening. A red cast clung to the evening sky. Might be a good time for a late-night surf. Maybe he could talk Cole into coming along. The buddy system was always best, and Max was nothing if not cautious.

Or maybe he should just go home and pull his profile off every one of these services.

No point in wasting any more of his valuable time.

He drove home, his thoughts on Ava. She'd suggested that he pretend to be her boyfriend at her upcoming family birthday dinner. The idea wasn't really crazy and wouldn't be a waste of his time. Maybe they could arrange a trade of some kind. He decided then and there that he was going to take her up on the invitation.

This *wasn't* because Ava intrigued him. No, he had to reject that theory outright. But he wouldn't mind spending at least one evening with her. Simply a test, to find out if she had an off switch.

He refused to entertain the idea that he was interested in Ava. That attraction was purely physical, and he understood animal magnetism more than most.

And it wasn't ridiculous to want something deeper.

Chapter Four

On Monday morning, Ava unlocked the office of the Chamber of Commerce. They were located smack-dab in the middle of downtown next to the Charming Community Bank. Redbrick siding and the US flag next to the Texas one distinguished it from being just another business. Inside the small office she had a desk, computer monitor, printer, and dozens of pamphlets and Charming city maps featuring area businesses. She had her second French press, and a tub of her personally roasted beans in an airtight plastic container. But every morning she made coffee for one, unless she had an appointment with a new business owner in town, in which case she made enough for two.

Everyone raved about her coffee, asking where they could buy some.

She settled in for a slow morning, composed of any last-minute fires she might have to put out. Last week, the website had inexplicably stopped working and refused to allow her to log in. She regularly updated a welcome post on the front page and had a small stroke when she couldn't. Several hours on the phone with their hosting company, she had an update to their plug-ins, and was back in business.

Please, no more fires to put out.

This was her birthday week, after all, and she had enough to contend with, what with her family coming to torture her.

She checked her email and responded to several inquiries about joining the Chamber of Commerce and how that might help their business thrive. This was where Ava went into her sales mode. But truthfully, a business would do fine without the fanfare of their big ribbon-cutting ceremonies and their annual Mr. Charming contest, in which a business owner or employee could win a cash prize to do with as they pleased. Most upgraded their storefronts, but many used it for personal reasons. To Ava, the Chamber was really about community, like so many other things that mattered in a small town. She was here to support any business owner who needed her because everyone could use a cheerleader.

She went over a few last-minute details on the mayor's anniversary party a little over a week from now. When there was a lull in the morning, Ava pulled out her business plan and looked it over. This version had been rejected by their own local bank. Bill, the loan officer, had been close to tears when he'd given Ava the bad news. She'd actually wound up consoling him.

Maybe if she made a few changes here and there. She rummaged through her top drawer for her red pen.

The glass door swung open, and Ava looked up, smile ready. "Welcome to… Oh hi, Max."

"Hey."

He was dressed in board shorts and a Salty Dog T-shirt. Ava rarely saw him this dressed down. His wavy dark hair was slightly windblown and for the first time she noticed the natural copper highlights. It appeared he hadn't shaved, and Max always shaved. His skin was sun-kissed and bronzed. He might have just come from the beach. She got a good look at his sinewy biceps, the cords in his forearms bunching.

Over a year ago when Max and Cole had taken over the Salty Dog, it had been Max who'd come down to sign them up for a membership. Even then, he'd been dressed for success in slacks and a white button-up. No tie. He'd warmly shaken her hand and told her how important it was to him to be part of a small-town business community. Ava realized that Max and Cole didn't need to be chamber members for their continued success as a historic location and the only bar in the town. But Max, like her, thought it was important.

Stuffing the business plan back in her top desk drawer, she folded her hands. "What can I do for you?"

He took a seat. "It's more what I can do for you."

Her skin tightened at the sweet sound of his words. "*That* sounds intriguing."

"Do you still need a date to your birthday dinner?"

Ava hesitated. To answer yes implied she had no one else interested in her. Pretty sad.

And Max didn't have to know that she'd recently noticed he was hotter than Texas asphalt. She'd explained that she only wanted him for his résumé.

"Yes. I've had lots of offers, but like I said, I wanted someone to *impress* my family."

"And I'm flattered that you would consider me." He gave her a brief smile.

"Why? Are you suddenly available?"

She would *not* allow herself to believe that Max could like her. She'd known him for over a year and he'd never expressed the slightest interest. But the mere idea sent little slivers of heat pulsing through her.

"I'd love to go to dinner with your family." He waited a beat. "And I hope you can return the favor."

"Y-you want me to go to dinner with your family?" Her heart beat hard enough to hear the thudding sound in her ears.

"No, but I have another idea."

Her palms grew sweaty and she leaned forward.

Truth be told, Ava wouldn't mind a boyfriend. She hadn't dated anyone seriously in years. A few months ago, she'd been attracted to Cole, who only liked her as a friend. Cole was so approachable, so kind, such a friendly flirt, and so…safe. But Max…well, he scared her a little bit. He wasn't particularly friendly and certainly not approachable.

Now that fear drummed down her legs in little aching throbs and she recognized it was becoming something entirely different. Excitement.

Magnetic attraction, pure and simple.

"I'm going to drop out of these online dating services. What I need is someone who knows me, and someone I trust. I immediately thought of you."

Yes, yes, yes!

She wanted to throw herself over the desk, and into his arms, and claim that of course she'd date him! Those arms would be so warm, and she could almost feel the prickly sensation of his skin on hers. The beard stubble against her neck.

"Max…" She cocked her head and smiled, a little shy.

This was happening so quickly, but she'd heard that sometimes love happened this way. Valerie said the moment she'd first laid eyes on Cole, even though they'd been teenagers, she just…knew. And then, a mere fourteen years later, they were about to get married.

The moral? Never give up.

"It just makes sense. You have so many contacts.

You're the heart of this town. And I think you should find me the perfect match."

If her head was a balloon, this was when it would pop. Her neck jerked back.

"Huh? Wh-what?"

"I'll go to your birthday dinner, and in exchange, you find the perfect woman to be my future wife."

"The perfect woman." She cleared her throat. "There is no perfect woman."

"You know what I mean. Perfect for me." He stretched his legs in front of him and crossed his arms. "You've seen my résumé."

Her spine tensed. Spare her from a man who thought he could achieve love like he'd achieved his business success. Max was seriously beginning to piss her off.

"And what does your résumé have to do with finding love?"

"I need someone like me. Driven, ambitious, career oriented. Serious. You get the gist."

"And will actual affection, or tenderness of any type, figure into this scenario?" If Ava had a pencil, she'd snap it in half.

"That's the part I'm having a difficult time with. Personality. People are lying on these services and I don't have time for that."

"Look at my face." She pointed. "Shock."

"You know about the first woman. On the second date, a grandmother showed up to screen her granddaughter's dates. The third woman got up every ten minutes to brush her teeth. The fourth woman couldn't even look me in the eye and said two words to me all night. She was *terrified* of me."

He'd had four dates in three days! "You do have a slightly intimidating look about you."

"What's so intimidating about me? I'm big, but so is Cole."

"You remember the shaken-not-stirred reference? Can you actually kill someone with your finger? Because you look like you would happily do it."

He scrunched his eyebrows. "What does that mean? You think I look like a hired *assassin*?"

"Face it, you're a grump."

"Am not."

"Oh, puhleeze." She crossed her arms.

"Okay, I'm in a bad mood sometimes. But people are stupid."

"And that's no reason to be *mean*."

"Not everyone can be as happy as you are with a simple ribbon-cutting ceremony."

Ouch. That hurt. He sounded vaguely like her older brother James, the snob.

A ribbon-cutting ceremony. How quaint.

"Sounds vaguely grumpy, Mr. Grump. Because I'm such a cheerful person, that means I have a boatload of friends. Think about it."

"I have, and that's why I'm here. What do you say?"

"You'll go to my birthday dinner, pretend to be my boyfriend and impress my parents. And all I have to do is find you the perfect wife. It doesn't sound like an equal trade-off." She made a face. "One is for a single night, and I'll find you a lifetime of happiness."

He nodded. "Fair point. Anything else I can do for you?"

The thought came to Ava swiftly. "Now that you mention it, I could use a little help with my business plan."

"Let me see it."

"Now?" She wasn't ready.

Maybe he'd make fun of her plans. A few changes here and there and she might be ready to show it to Mr. Smarty-Pants. She still had to present it as the final project in her business class and maybe get some more suggestions there.

"Sure. I'll take it home and give it a read tonight."

A small part of Ava wanted to keep her plan buried in the desk drawer where it would be safe from ridicule. But she'd come to understand that if she wanted her dream to come true, she might have to accept a little constructive criticism along the way.

Little rivulets of fear ran down her spine as she pulled it out of the drawer. It felt as if she was handing over her precious baby to a big, bad monster.

"Be nice."

He quirked a brow. "Be *nice* or give you solid advice? Which would you prefer?"

"Um…solid advice."

"Good answer." He flipped through the papers, appearing to scan them briefly. "A coffee shop."

Every muscle in her body tensed to granite and she got ready to swing and fight. To give him hell for making fun of her. It was one thing for her family to ridicule her, another thing for Max. They weren't related by blood and she'd be damned if she'd put up with it. Uh-uh. No way.

"Yes. Is that a problem?" She crossed her arms.

"No." He squinted. "You mean just because there are three others in town?"

"I have a plan."

"You'll need one."

She snorted. "Since we're busy stepping on dreams, why do *you* want to get *married*?"

"Does it matter?"

"It does to me if I'm going to fix you up with any of the classmates from my graduating Princeton class. I care about these women."

"You went to *Princeton*?" He gaped.

"Don't look so shocked. My parents wouldn't have it any other way. Since I was enrolled in SAT prep courses from the time I was ten, I did okay."

"Ten? Wow. Even I wouldn't do that to my kids."

"So, you want kids."

"Look, I'm thirty-four, and it's time to settle down. I'm ready to be a father, and everything *about* me is ready. My financial outlook. My future, secure. My heart, open. I stopped sleeping with random women a year ago. And I have a lot to offer the right woman."

Ava fanned herself. "This is all so romantic. I'm getting a little hot. And how's your IRA?"

He scowled. "These things are important in a solid marriage. And my IRA is well padded."

"What about love?" Great, she sounded like a song.

"I'm sure that will come in time if I'm with the right woman. But I have to start with compatibility. Once we meet, there should be sparks. Or something."

It sounded as if he were ordering a meal. *Add some sparks in, would you, a little chemistry on the side?* "Who knows? Maybe with the right woman, you won't care so much about her stock shares. I'm just thinking out loud here."

He didn't miss her sarcasm. "Are you going to do this or not? I could ask Valerie, but she's worse than you are when it comes to romance. I trust you more, especially now that I know you graduated from Princeton. You *must* be smart."

Attraction to this man had become a distant memory.

He was callous, arrogant, and she wondered if, like the Tin Man, he didn't really have a heart. "Fine! I'll do it."

He stood. "Text me the details of dinner. I promise before the night is done your family will be impressed."

"I have no doubt, Romeo."

He walked out the door, taking her plan with him,

and leaving Ava fuming. She'd just met the real Max, the worst male specimen she'd ever known. He might be a savvy entrepreneur, but he would make someone a horrible husband.

She watched as outside, he stood at the crosswalk, head bent, waiting for the light to change. When Mrs. Barrett came around the corner from the store carrying two paper bags, he took both from her, tucking the business plan under one arm. Then he crossed the street with Mrs. Barrett, still not smiling, while the elderly woman tucked her arm in his.

Okay, so maybe not the *worst* man on earth.

Chapter Five

Ava found exactly the right woman for Max and he probably deserved her.

She and Mercedes Ewing sat in a booth at the Salty Dog, a venue Mercedes had immediately declared perfectly adequate, though rustic. Ava had made sure to sit them at Valerie's table, who was working a shift tonight.

Valerie happened to be the best waitress here, even if she was actually a third-grade teacher who only filled in as needed now. Point being, she was also Ava's best friend, and would be her eyes and ears tonight. Max had asked Ava to make herself scarce after introductions, and he'd take it from there.

"I can't believe it's been five years since we

spoke," Mercedes Ewing said, sipping her cosmo. "I see your family regularly at all the big charity galas."

"Thanks for making the drive. I think this will be worthwhile."

"I thought you were still mad at me."

"Nah, don't be silly. I didn't need that gap year."

When Ava had confided that she was planning on a gap year between high school and college, Mercedes personally went to Ava's parents and made the case for why this was such a bad idea. Not that she had to do much convincing with the Longs. More like alerting. Ava's plans had been dead in the water before she even approached her parents with her plan.

Ava had attended private school with Mercedes, but she hadn't attended Princeton. She'd been to *Yale* and graduated summa cum laude. They didn't come brighter and shinier than Mercedes, who, while not beautiful, was cute with short auburn hair that she kept perfectly coiffed. She had a law degree from Harvard and, as her mother never failed to mention, now worked in Houston as one of a cluster of attorneys who defended a major high-tech company's rights to a virtual monopoly whenever *that* came into question.

Mercedes believed in planning, hard work and little else, from what Ava had been able to discern in all the years she'd known her.

"I'm looking forward to this. There are so few good men out there. I haven't had a date in two years. Most men are afraid of me. Even my boss." She frowned.

"From what I know of you and Max, I think you'll be a perfect fit."

"Is he good-looking?" Her eyes flitted to Cole behind the bar, mixing it up, both cocktail-wise and with customers. "Like him. I've never seen a better-looking bartender, in a plebian sort of way."

And that was the thing about Mercedes. She used words like *plebian* and *gauche* in daily conversation.

"Max is extremely good-looking, and I know how important that is to you."

"He doesn't have to be perfect, as long as he's fastidious about his appearance."

"I've never seen him sloppy or unkempt."

"You've definitely done a wonderful job of selling him. But I don't understand why he can't get a date."

"He could probably ask any woman in here and they'd fall at his feet. The point is, he doesn't want just anyone. He wants someone special. That's why I thought of you."

She was also using Mercedes as a yardstick. And maybe it was time for Max to learn a lesson. If he looked in a mirror, he might not like what he saw, metaphorically speaking. It was a puzzle, because from everything she'd heard from Cole about Max's family, they couldn't be more different than him. Happy people who sucked the marrow out of life with their Latin food, dance and music. It was almost as if Max had been born into the family Ava should have.

Just then Max walked inside the bar, scanned the room and immediately fixated on them. He weaved his way through some of the regulars, shaking hands as he was stopped, and moving with his ultimate confidence, assuredness and ease.

"Oh. My. God," Mercedes said. "Is that him?"

Oh boy. Max did look especially handsome tonight, dressing down this time in dark jeans and a white button-up rolled up to his forearms. No tie, but he'd shaved.

"That's Max. He went casual tonight. Too bad, because he can really rock a suit."

"I'm sorry I doubted you. I honestly thought you might still be angry with me after all these years."

"Are you serious? I wouldn't do that to you!"

But she would do it to Max. *This* anger was new and fresh. What was it that Nanny Lucia always used to say?

La vengansa es un plato que se sirve frio.

Revenge is a plate best served cold.

Max required a wake-up call, and Ava would be the one to deliver it. She rose slightly to wave him over, even if he'd already seen them, and was casually making his way in their direction.

"Hey," Max said with all the smooth finesse of a dark woodsy espresso. "I'm Max Del Toro."

Ava stood to let Max take her place on the bench seat and Valerie returned a moment later.

"Can I refresh that cosmo for you?" Valerie asked.

"No, thank you, I'm fine." Mercedes's eyes were riveted to Max.

Ava cleared her throat. "Max, this is my dear friend Mercedes Ewing. She's from Dallas but lives and works in Houston now."

"It's nice to meet you, Mercedes."

"Well, I'll just leave you two to get to know each other." Ava walked away, listening to Valerie ask whether they'd like menus.

She could just leave right now, but gosh, she didn't want to miss the show. She went to the bar, where she took a seat near the place Cole filled drink orders and ordered her usual coffee and Kahlua. She'd never hurt Cole's feelings, but the coffee they served here tasted as though it had been strained through lettuce leaves. The only way she could drink any was with the help of some of their best liqueur. Often, Ava wondered whether she should offer some of her own roasted beans, but that might indicate there was something seriously wrong with the Salty Dog's coffee. She didn't want to hurt anyone's feelings.

Cole set down her coffee and Kahlua. "Don't you ever drink anything but coffee?"

"I love my beans. But I've been known to drink a beer or two from time to time. I want to stay perfectly sober tonight, though, and enjoy the show."

Cole gave her his dimpled smile. "What show?"

"Oh, just that moment when Max sees himself in the mirror."

He quirked a brow, poor man. Cole didn't know about Ava's slightly devious side. No one did. Every few minutes, Ava stole furtive glances in their direction. Max was doing a lot of listening and nodding, but he smiled too, which was unusual. Did he actually...*like* Mercedes? Regret pierced her and she felt like she'd been kicked in the gut. She hadn't been prepared for him to *like* her. If he did, he and Mercedes would be married within six months and she'd be invited to their high society wedding.

Within nine months, Mercedes would have their first perfectly timed baby, followed closely by the exact sibling spacing Mercedes would have researched. She wouldn't really love Max because she wasn't capable of loving anyone but herself. And Ava would be forced to go to bed every night knowing she'd done this to a man who helped little ladies cross the street when he thought no one was watching.

Because there was something oddly intriguing about this man who claimed he wanted a completely different life than the one Ava did. Something in his dark gaze pulled her to him and made her believe he hid a secret from the rest of the world. There was something much deeper about the man than his portfolio and numerous achievements.

Valerie sidled up with her tray and placed some orders, which Cole immediately went to mix.

"How's it going so far?" Ava whispered.

"She's interesting, isn't she?"

"You can say it. She's a snob."

Valerie went hand on hip and tossed her hair. "Your friend, a snob?"

"Um, yes. And she's not really my friend. Just an old classmate. I thought it might be good for Max to see how he comes off to others. To Mercedes, *spontaneity* is a dirty word. She's planned every minute of her life." She glanced at the clock behind the bar, in the shape of a bulldog. "Let's see, she's twenty-nine, so she's on the clock to have her first child within a year or so. She better get crackin'."

"Oh boy. Sounds like I missed that deadline." Valerie shimmied her shoulders. "Cole hasn't knocked me up yet. Not sure what he's waitin' for. Hurry up, baby!"

He quickly set two IPA beers on her tray. "Comin' right up with the margarita. Don't rush me, woman."

Ava and Valerie turned to each other and burst into laughter.

"Now that I can speak freely," Valerie said. "She's making Nick jump through hoops tonight. Everything is special order."

"And she'll complain privately that places this plebian can't ever get a steak right. It's in the cut of meat, you see. Only the finest and most exclusive of restaurants pay top dollar for the choice Angus beef," Ava said in her best haughty, high society matron snob imitation.

"Well, she better not say that to Max. He's personally arranged for us to have a contract with DeWitt Meats and they're the best."

"Oh! Wait. Best of all? She doesn't know that Max owns this restaurant. I just told her he was a handsome businessman ready to settle down. I can't wait to see what—"

"Ava."

She didn't have to turn around to know Max had come up behind her.

Chapter Six

"Hey." Ava swiveled on her stool to face him. "What's up? You two havin' a good time?"

Max was gratified to catch the wary look in her green eyes. Because if she didn't already feel bad enough about this disaster, he would help get her there. She'd just fixed him up with the worst date of his life. Mercedes Ewing was a first-rate snob, and they were about as well suited to each other as steak and ketchup.

"No."

She looked over his shoulder, presumably to find Mercedes. "Where—"

"She left. When she complained about the meal and said the quality of her steak was crude, I let her know I own this place. Which, apparently, is something *you* never told her."

"Um, well, I—"

"Seriously?"

"Look, I'm sorry it's not a love match. I just wanted you to see how—"

"Come here," he said, offering his hand to help her down.

She took his hand and he kept a tight hold as he led her through the crowded bar outside for a little one-on-one privacy. They would have to straighten this out one way or another. Since they spent a lot of time together, mostly due to Cole and Valerie, they had to keep the peace. But right now, he wanted to chew her out. He didn't appreciate the obvious prank at his expense. She'd wasted *more* of his time.

Outside, the October evening was mild, and the rolling waves calm and quiet. A seagull squawked and Ava jumped.

"Is this where you kill me with your finger?"

"What are you *talking* about?"

"Never mind."

He wanted to cut her up into little shreds of ribbon with his words but was distracted by the shaft of moonlight glinting off her pale blond hair. Her pouty lower lip seemed to quiver, or was that his imagination? She looked ten times more beautiful than Mercedes. He ignored the pull of attraction and the magnetism he felt whenever around her. He would also ignore that, at the moment, he strongly suspected she might be shaking. No words out of her now. Instead, a quiet calm. A strange feeling of tenderness surged through him, like that time he'd rescued an abandoned dog left on the streets of Dallas.

He wouldn't think about that right now. Or ever. No room for any other emotion here but anger. No one wasted his time.

He had to set Ava straight on a few things about him. Because first and foremost, they were friends, and colleagues.

"Is this what you think of me? You think *I'm* a snob?"

"No." She crossed her arms. "I think you're like Mercedes in that you're incapable of being spontaneous."

"You don't think I can be *spontaneous*? That's insane. I can be spontaneous. All over the damn place, if I want."

"Really? What's the last unplanned thing you did?"

He didn't move, considering. Once upon a time, he'd taken bigger risks. But even those had been calculated. Risk tolerance was key, and you didn't become a navy SEAL without being willing to take risks. But spontaneous? Hell no. He'd have been laughed off his team. He lived by a plan. Then and now. The past few years stateside had been about finishing his degree, starting and selling businesses, and making money so that he'd never need to take charity the way his parents had. So that his wife and children would never want for anything.

"It's smart to plan in business, and you're savvy there. But with love, with attraction, sometimes you just have to take a risk."

While he understood that, he didn't see why it was so wrong to begin with compatibility first. Then, the last missing piece would have to be there, too. Obviously. He would need that certain tug of desire like the one that made him want to take Ava home and shower her with his spontaneity. All night long.

In this case, the attraction was unexplainable to him beyond the physical. And he really wanted to believe he'd gotten past making decisions based solely on physical attraction. He still hadn't responded to the question, going over it in his mind and coming up with zip. Pathetic.

"You're still trying to remember *one* moment, aren't you?"

"When's the last time *you* were spontaneous?"

"That would be this past July at the Chamber cookout when Tom asked me to get up and sing 'American Pie' with him and his band." She held up air quotes on the word band. "I don't know all the words, and there are a lot of words."

"Why would you do something like that?"

She shrugged. "Fun. Fake it till you make it."

That didn't make any sense to him. A person couldn't *fake* something and actually make it happen. Trust him on this. But there might be some female subtlety that he'd missed.

Her eyes narrowed. "And you're still trying to think of just one thing, huh?"

There had been only one crazy thought on his mind lately, one he'd never acted on. Which meant the very *opposite* of what they were talking about, but he wasn't going to go there. Let her think the idea had just occurred to him. He might just be losing his mind a little bit, because something inside him came apart. Just cracked wide-open.

You want spontaneous? I'll show you spontaneous, baby.

He moved closer to her and wrapped his palm around the nape of her neck, meeting her gaze. She blinked in surprise, but her eyes never wavered from his own and in them he saw the softness of a clear invitation. Even so, he moved slowly, pulling her close, hip to hip, waiting for her to tell him to stop this foolery. Giving her plenty of time. But she didn't say a damn word. He waited for her to flinch. To move his hand from the curve of her ass.

Instead she lowered her gaze to his lips.

Because, of course, this was Ava before him. Open for fun, and impulsive kisses. Casual. That person wasn't him, not anymore, but now at least for this moment, it could be. Oh, hell yeah.

He met her lips, warm and sweet. She tasted like a fine liqueur, exactly how he'd imagined she would. One kiss and he stopped and met her gaze. In those shimmering eyes, he saw surprise mixed with desire, and it lit him on fire. He kissed her again, harder this time, and she opened for him, thrusting her warm tongue into his mouth. Her fingers were threading through his hair, and he didn't know what she was doing to him, but he went from zero to a hundred in a single moment. This worked for him.

It worked a little too well because he had to remind himself that this *wasn't* the plan.

With heat pulsating through him, and breaths a little uneven, he managed to pull away and make his point. "How's *that* for spontaneous?"

"Yeah," she breathed. "That was so good I didn't even see it coming."

Me, either.

And that made more than heat throb through him. This time traces of an emotion he'd learned to manage well hit him hard and fast. Fear, raw and real. Adrenaline pumping at Mach 2 levels. His heart told him there was something here with Ava worth exploring. But his brain told him otherwise, and whenever those two were in disagreement, his brain won every single time. That process had gotten him out of the picking fields of Watsonville and to the man he was today.

Ava was a young twenty-eight to his thirty-four, and flighty. Her enthusiasm was over-the-top at times. She reminded him of a thousand-watt bulb in a reading lamp. Too much. He couldn't imagine living with her day in and day out. Okay, so maybe he was a bit of a grump. She was right about that.

"It's good that we did this." Max cleared his throat. "If I'm supposed to be your boyfriend at your birthday dinner, we should at least be comfortable with each other."

She cast her eyes down and wouldn't look at him. "Good point."

He stepped back. "Now you know I can be spontaneous. Next time find me someone with a little personality."

"Next time?"

"You're going to give up that easily? Or do you really want to force me back to those ridiculous services?"

"No, I wouldn't want that." She chewed on her lower lip. "It's just that…"

"Yeah?"

He half hoped she'd tell him to give up, that she wanted him for herself.

Face it, genius. You wouldn't turn her down even if you're not on the same page. Not even the same book.

They could only be together if this was Ava's idea. If she could meet him halfway. Because if she didn't want him to find someone else, she might be forced to explore why. Whether that was good or bad for him, the sooner he knew, the sooner he could get Ava off his mind and move on.

Especially after that kiss.

"I just…don't know what you want, other than personality, and a good résumé."

"What if I make you a list?"

She crossed her arms. "A list?"

"A list of what I'm looking for in a woman."

"I'm beginning to regret that kiss. If you have double Ds on your list, I'm going to light it on fire."

"Ha. That's how little you know me." He tipped back on his heels. "I'm an ass and legs man."

She went palms up. "Give me your stupid list and if I'm still talking to you after I read it, I'll see what I can do."

The next night was Ava's birthday dinner. It took a special alignment of the stars and planets to get four doctors together on one night, so it wasn't as if Ava could back out. Their schedules had been firmed up a year in advance. Since approximately her last birthday dinner. To cancel now would cause absolute chaos in her family. It was simply out of the question. Even Max would be upset, as he'd also set the night aside and lord knew how *he* loved his plans.

Meanwhile, Ava would love a drive along the coast tonight. Or perhaps a movie at the Granada. She'd heard great things about the new romantic comedy out now. None of that would happen tonight. She had an obligation. It was her twenty-ninth birthday. Yay.

She took another look at Max's list on her phone. He'd texted it to her later the same night of his epic fail with Mercedes. Even though the list depressed Ava, she'd read it several times that day.

Between the ages of 30-36
Intelligent
Kind and compassionate
Well educated—at least a bachelor's but more is better here
Even-tempered, not easily excitable
Quiet and introverted
Highly successful in her career and/or business
Brunette
Ready for marriage and children

She sighed. "How can a man who kisses a woman the way he did be this lame?"

Another thing she did far more often than check this ridiculous list: relive that kiss. Every detail. The surf had been crashing in the background, the seagulls squawking, the wind whistling. He'd confidently reached for her and tugged her into his arms. His kiss was commanding, just like him. Consuming. Hot. Pretty unforgettable.

And then he'd texted her The List, saying he'd add more if he thought of anything.

It was almost as if he'd literally taken every character trait of Ava's and asked for the opposite. Except for the education, intelligence and compassion, she didn't make a single item on his list. She didn't even meet the age requirement!

By the way, an *age requirement*? But the one that hurt her the most was the "successful in her career or business." Ava was neither. By now, she should have been a lot further along in her plans, but something always stopped her.

A location she'd scoped out suddenly became unavailable. The price of coffee beans shot up. A business loan wasn't approved.

She lost her nerve.

She glanced at the rainbow clock on her kitchen wall. Max would arrive at her cottage imminently, no doubt, right on time. Which was why she'd given him a time fifteen minutes past when they were to meet her parents at Le Oranguan. She was always fashionably late, a way of letting her parents know no matter what, she was still in control of her own life. It drove them all batty, though by now they should expect it. One year, they'd moved the time later, and she'd still been fifteen minutes late. Were it up to Max, they'd probably be early. She couldn't have that. This was still her show.

She'd spent most of her birthday roasting beans and consulting the many notes she'd accumulated over the years. She'd been experimenting with mixing different flavors in with the beans. Today, she'd tried a cinnamon nutmeg blend for an autumn-like flavor. After lunch she'd surfed Pinterest. Thanksgiving was already next month, and after Black Friday, the days would pass in a whirlwind of shopping and eating.

The doorbell rang, precisely on time, of course. Ava made the final touches to her hair and went to open the door. There stood Max in his dark suit, looking as though he'd stepped off the pages of *GQ* magazine.

Oh, sigh. If only he didn't talk.

"Right on time."

He squinted. "What's that in your hair?"

"My tiara?" She touched it briefly. "I wear it every year on my birthday."

"Where everyone can *see* you?"

"Yes, *Max*. That's the point. I'm the birthday girl." She grabbed her purse and joined him outside.

The night was typical for the Gulf Coast in autumn, cool, but never too cold. It was her favorite time of the year.

Max opened the passenger door to his silver convertible car. "You look lovely."

"You don't have to say that."

"I know, but I mean it."

"Thanks, then."

Tonight, she'd gone with her Audrey Hepburn *Breakfast at Tiffany's* look. It went well with the tiara. Sleek black A-line dress hitting just above the knee, and classic black strappy heels. On her birthday, she tried to give her mother something, so she usually dressed in the elegant and sophisticated way of the woman that she was not. It was the least she could do for the woman she'd disappointed so much simply by being herself.

"You should know, we're running a little late," Ava said.

"What? Why?" He glanced at his wristwatch. "I'm right on time."

"Don't worry, my family is used to this. I'm always fifteen minutes late. It's my thing."

He scowled. "Damn it, Ava, being late is *not* how I impress people."

"Don't worry, you're not going to have any trouble impressing my family. I've already told them about you. I've paved the way."

"Okay, let's go over a few things first. Remind me again who I'm meeting tonight. Your mother, Dr. Katherine Long, your father Dr. William Long, and your brothers, right? Both doctors."

"My brothers, Dr. James Long, and Dr. Robert Long. Their wives, Angelica and Makayla Long. And since I haven't said so yet, please let me apologize for tonight in advance."

"Why would you do that? I agreed to this."

"If you thought that Mercedes was a snob…"

"I'm sure they can't be *that* bad."

"If you say so." She clicked her seat belt into place, the sound loud in the cocoon of the closed, top-up convertible. Wonder if Max ever drove it with the top down. "Um, have you had a chance to look at my business plan yet?"

"I was going to talk to you about that tonight." Max pulled out onto the highway.

She took a shallow breath, steeling herself against

the questionable wisdom of yet another coffee shop when there were already so many, at least one which dominated the market with their chain stores from coast to coast.

"Let me have your advice."

"You're in the perfect town, actually, to open up a coffee shop if that's what you want to do. As you well know, the mayor and city council of Charming aren't allowing the big-box stores, or any large chain, to lease space in town. I should know, because I'd like the Salty Dog to be a franchise, so I've researched their regulations."

Excitement bubbled up and she jumped a little in her seat. "You *like* my idea?"

"Calm down. If this is what you want to do, and if your heart is set on it, I think you should do it."

"You? *You* think I should do it?"

Ava didn't want to say so, but this was a little like the Grinch agreeing Christmas was a good idea. If she wasn't sitting down, she'd get up and dance.

"Why does that surprise you?"

"Because of Starbucks, for one. There are tons of them in our neighboring cities. And there are already other coffee shops in town."

"Don't get me wrong. I think every entrepreneur should study the Starbucks business model. Don't you think there were plenty of coffee shops around before them? What they built was a brand. And that's what everyone in business *should* do in order to be successful."

"A brand."

Not for the first time, Ava wished she'd gone to business school, instead of getting the political science degree her parents had talked her into. They claimed there would be a lot of reading, which she thoroughly enjoyed, and they knew it. At the time, she had been shiftless, and uncertain about her future.

Now she was trying to play catch-up by taking courses at the community college.

"From what I read in your business plan you already have something special to offer that makes your coffee experience unique."

"My beans. I learned the best way to roast them from an expert. I really do have to fix you a cup of coffee soon. You won't believe what a difference the right kind of beans, freshly roasted, can make."

"Do many coffee places roast their beans on the premises?"

"Some have in the past. I don't know that any of them do right now. They usually have a roasting plant off-site."

"Probably for volume." Max expertly pulled his convertible to the curbside valet parking. "But if you stick to roasting the beans on-site, that already makes your space more unique."

Max climbed out and met her on the passenger side. They both headed toward the entrance to the restaurant.

She walked ahead, until Max reached for her hand

and pulled her back to him. "Wait. How long have we known each other?"

"I told my mother we've been dating for three months."

"All right. If there's anything we don't know, and they ask, let's cover for each other."

"Sure," she said, not surprised he'd thought that far ahead.

So had she. At three months, they could still be learning things about each other.

Ironic that she was pretend dating a man who was everything her parents would want for her. Her past boyfriends had been free spirits, bohemian types that her family abhorred. She'd dated them precisely for that reason.

But for the first time, her date was someone she might even want for herself, if only she hadn't seen his List. Max took her hand and confidently led her to the restaurant and toward the maître d'. He walked with authority, as if this was *his* dinner, *his* reservations. It occurred to her that he always acted as though everything was his.

Tonight, that included her.

Chapter Seven

"We're here for the Long party," Max said.

Ava bit her lower lip and tried to squash a laugh. She wanted to make a joke about a long party, such as the miserable two hours they were likely to spend here tonight. But she would behave herself. No overt displays of affection, dial back on the wattage, take her cue from her boring sisters-in-law. Always an exhausting evening.

This was all easier to do when she'd already asserted herself by being late, and by wearing the birthday tiara that annoyed her family. As they approached the table, Ava caught sight of her father first. He sat pensively stroking his white goatee, no doubt deep in thought about a patient. She hadn't seen him in six months, and her heart ached because he looked so much older than he had the last time. He worked too hard, cared too much. She wanted to launch herself into her daddy's arms the way she had when she was a little girl, but he'd stopped accepting that kind of public affection long ago.

All three men stood as Ava approached, even if James always seemed annoyed to do it, scowling and readjusting his tie. Granted, if she'd been here on time none of them would have had to stand, so he had a point. Another perk of being late.

It had become difficult to ignore Max's hand firmly around her waist. She turned to him.

"Everyone, this is Max Del Toro. My b-boyfriend… that I told you about."

Brutal men's handshakes were exchanged all around and introductions made. No hugs, of course. Ava noted that Mikayla, one of her sisters-in-law, was missing.

"Mikayla couldn't make it," Robert said, at the same time as he reached inside his coat pocket and handed Ava an envelope. "Happy birthday, sis."

Almost simultaneously all the men reached inside their pockets and handed Ava an envelope.

"Thanks so much," Ava said.

Granted, she would have preferred a heartfelt gift but had stopped hoping. They thought by giving her cash they were funding her shopping habits, when every dollar they gave her went into her coffee shop dream fund.

"Tell them why Mikayla couldn't make it, Robert," her mother said proudly, but then went ahead and said it for him anyway. "Andrew is the youngest ever to make it into the National Spelling Bee finals. They had to go to Maryland this weekend for the first round."

"He's *five*," Ava said.

Not to mention the last time she'd visited, little Andrew seemed to have a big biting problem.

"Isn't it incredible?" her mother said. "Youngest ever. The second-youngest, a girl, was six. She eventually got disqualified because she couldn't pass the written test."

"Fascinating," Max said to Robert. "You must be so proud."

"Did Ava tell you she was once a finalist in the National Spelling Bee championship? We're more of a math and science family, Max, but our little Ava has always been unique."

"I was ten. I think I've done more than the National Spelling Bee championship with my life."

"I know, dear. I'm just using it as an example of your many achievements. I know you don't like to brag, but these are things Max should know about you. Max, why don't you tell us more about yourself?"

Ava expected Max to launch into a dissertation on his career in the navy, followed by his education, degrees and stock portfolio. To her surprise, he didn't.

Instead, he went into a lengthy discussion on how

he and his business partner had saved the Salty Dog from bankruptcy when they'd taken it over last year. He talked about how he'd joined the Chamber of Commerce figuring it was something he should do, and that Ava had been welcoming and encouraging to a new business owner.

"She's everybody's cheerleader," Max finished. "I don't know what the city would do without her. I know the mayor thinks of Ava as her right-hand woman."

This was an incredible exaggeration, but Ava sure appreciated it.

"I always thought Ava had a gift of persuasion, which is why I encouraged her to go into law," Mom continued. "I can see now that the job at the Chamber has been like a stepping-stone. You might be a good fit for politics, Ava."

Ava nearly spit her water out. And for the first time in the evening, her father perked up. He'd never been fond of lawyers and considered politicians not much better than dirt.

"Katherine, don't be ridiculous. I won't have *my* daughter making her living by schlepping around begging for votes."

"I'm talking small-town politics, dear."

Maybe this might be a good time to remind them all about the coffee shop because she wasn't throwing her hat into the political arena.

"I'm still planning to start my own business. That's where my heart is."

Dad simply closed his eyes and rubbed his forehead like he had a headache coming on. James and Robert consulted their pagers. Angelica played with her diamond-studded necklace.

Mom pursed her lips in her I've-about-had-it-with-you look.

"You've been planning that for years," she said. "When is this going to actually happen?"

Four years. She'd come up with the idea after spending a year in Colombia with Nanny Lucia. That gap year? She'd taken it *after* graduating from Princeton. One glorious year of Latin food, roasting coffee beans, music and the carefree life. Then she'd returned to Texas, looked for a job and come up with the idea to start her own coffee shop. She'd specifically researched small towns and found Charming to be very proactive for the small business owner.

"Soon." Ava tipped her chin. "I have a business plan and now I've got the ear of a very savvy businessman who's helping me address some concerns."

Beside her, Max draped his arm around her shoulders in a protective stance. He didn't have to say a word. Mom got the message.

"Max, please talk my daughter out of this foolish idea."

"It's not foolish, Mom!" She crossed her arms. "And please don't put Max in the middle."

"Not foolish? How about careless? Have you ever heard of *Starbucks*? Honey, they'll squash you like a bug and have fun doing it."

"Excuse me," Max said. "Do any of you remember the days before we started paying five dollars for a cup of coffee? No one would have believed in that business model less than me. But most didn't see the big picture. I believe every business can be successful if there's a plan in place. A lot of hard work. And Ava works harder than most people."

"Thank you." Ava met his eyes, hearing the sincerity in his voice.

"Can we please order now?" Her father said. "The waiter has been circling us like a shark."

"Dear lord, yes, please," James said.

"I could eat my left arm," Robert added.

"Leave it to the men to keep us on a tight food schedule," Mom said with a laugh.

Attention on Ava lightened during dinner. Max became engaged in conversation with Robert about football, of all things. They seemed to be getting along and sharing a few laughs. James and Dad were discussing aortas, as they expertly cut into their steaks, and Mom and Angelica were talking potty training. Little Eddie appeared ready to conquer potty training ahead of the curve.

"The minute they show any interest at all, take away the diaper. You'll be glad you did. You might have to go through a few accidents, believe me, but sixteen months is *not* too young. I don't care what the pediatricians say."

Her mother, though an ob-gyn, also dispensed child-rearing advice.

And in her family, one was never too young for anything, unless it involved being free to make your own decisions.

There was, of course, no cake or dessert. Not with two cardiologists at the dinner table. No singing, either, because that might call too much attention to them. It was also considered rather vulgar in her family. They did have the annual champagne toast to Ava.

Afterward, Ava got pulled into a rare hug from Mom as they all waited for their respective cars by the valet. "Honey, he's wonderful. And *so* handsome."

When the valet parked Max's convertible, silver with a black top, it drew admiring glances from the men. All doctors, they really loved their cars, and they were often clean enough to perform surgery on the seats. Well, she was exaggerating. A little.

"She's a beauty," Dad said, admiring Max's car. "Ava, how's the Beamer running these days?"

Max flashed her a look, half confusion, and half curiosity. He knew that she drove around town in an economical sedan. Her father had gifted Ava the BMW on her birthday two years ago, worried about her safety in anything below rigid German standards. At least, that's what she told herself, and not that he wanted her to drive a status symbol.

"Great...just great." She blew a kiss to her father as Max held the passenger door open for her and she slipped inside.

A moment later, Max joined her, buckling his seat belt and sliding her a smirk. "BMW?"

"Don't ask."

Max was *going* to ask. There were a few things disturbing him about tonight's dinner and the BMW was the least of them, but a good place for him to start. He took off, cruising easily onto the road, and stopping at a red light where he could give her his full attention.

"Where's the Beamer, Ava?"

"How do you know I'm not storing it in a garage somewhere?"

"And driving a Honda instead? What's the point?"

She sat next to him, hands folded on her lap, looking as un-Ava-like as he'd ever seen her. It killed him. The dress she'd worn tonight, gorgeous though it made her look, was understated. A little plain for Ava, who loved bright colors and sometimes wore every one of them at the same time.

"Max, you have to understand. My father cares about me, and the only way he can express that is to make sure that I'm driving a reliable car."

"Okay, that makes sense. And why *don't* you drive it?"

She sighed. "It's a very expensive car."

"I'm aware." The light changed and he shifted gears. "And where is it?"

"What's the fascination with my car?"

He didn't know, exactly, but realized he'd rubbed

on a raw and exposed nerve and wanted to understand. Normally, he'd write this off as unimportant.
Insignificant. But all night, he'd been tuned in to
Ava. Supporting, understanding. Playing the part
of the dutiful boyfriend, and quite well if he said so
himself. Now he wanted a few answers.

"Fine! I sold it. Traded it in for something reliable but inexpensive. The extra money went into my
business slush fund."

"You've been saving."

He admired that. Most children of well-to-do families didn't know how to save since they'd never had
to be frugal.

"For years. I mean this, Max. I want to be an entrepreneur. I want to call the shots, make my own
way. When I work hard, which I always do, I want
the results to be mine. My baby. I want the pride of
knowing I did this all myself and I want to give back
to the community, too. I've never wanted to work for
anybody else."

It sounded a lot like his own beginning.

But several things had bothered him tonight. He'd
never been to dinner with a family so unlike his
own loud, large, demonstrative one. But rather than
the relief he wanted to feel, the whole evening left
him feeling a little cold inside. He couldn't imagine
what it had done to Ava to get what he assumed were
checks for her birthday. It made him want to run out
and get her a sentimental gift.

It had also made him wonder if this was what he

had to look forward to in his own future. Because families shouldn't be the place where one crowed about achievements. It was one thing to celebrate milestones but quite another to make love conditional on them. And he couldn't shake the feeling that Ava had never really been loved the way she should have been. Unconditionally and without expectations.

This was one area where his own large family had truly excelled. Max's achievements weren't accomplished to gain the love and acceptance of his family. He'd worked hard all his life to make sure the rest of the world saw him the same way that his family did.

"What are you doing the rest of the evening?"

"You can just take me home." She turned to him, the hint of a smile on her full pink lips. "And thank you. I know you probably don't realize it, but you really impressed my family tonight. The criticism, believe it or not, was minimal for a change. They were distracted by you."

Hard to believe that had been a family birthday celebration. No singing, no cake. No hugs. Whenever he got home to California for his birthday, the party lasted a week. Loud salsa music, crazy dancing and way too much food.

She looked so dejected, hands folded on her lap, prim and proper. Damn. This wasn't Ava. An impostor sat next to him.

Trying to lighten the mood, he went for a bit of humor. "I thought your father was going to have a coronary when your mother suggested that you go into politics."

"I know, right? I mean, the things she comes up with. She's getting desperate."

"What do you usually do every year after dinner with the family?"

"For the past couple of years, I usually go straight home."

"That's no way to spend your birthday." He took a right turn at the last minute and headed to the only bakery in town, Sweet and Charming.

"You need cake."

Chapter Eight

Max couldn't let this night end without getting some cake into Ava. Later, he might take her for a walk along the beach. Or drinks at the Salty Dog. He had a bar, for crying out loud, and people sometimes literally came in *just* to celebrate their birthday.

At this point he'd do anything to wipe that solemn look off Ava's face. He wanted to hear her laugh with that soft little trill of hers. Speak loudly. Jump on a table. Anything. He couldn't drop her off at her house knowing her family had sucked the spirit right out of her.

"I'm overdressed for this," she said.

"So am I." He pulled into the empty parking space

in front of the brightly lit bakery sign shaped like a purple-and-pink cupcake. "But what the hell."

"This counts as spontaneous." She turned to him and gave him the first real smile of the night.

"I told you."

Hand low on her back, he steered her toward the entrance. Sally, the teenager behind the counter, didn't blink an eye at their clothing. In fact, the shop was pretty dead, and she appeared to be comatose. She wore the ridiculous hat which was supposed to be a slice of cake but looked more like a football fan wearing the cheese head. A pink-and-purple cheese head.

"Hi, Sally!" Ava called out as he held the door open for her to walk inside.

Bright and beaming, the Ava he knew was back.

"Hey, Ava," the teenager said. "What's with the tiara?"

"Oh, I—" She briefly touched it, almost as if she'd forgotten she wore a crown on her head.

"It's her birthday," Max finished for her.

"Oh, dude, then you get a free cupcake. Our birthday special."

"Make that two," Max said, and pulled out his wallet.

They settled on a plastic bench. Though they were overdressed, oddly this didn't feel uncomfortable or tense. Maybe because this wasn't a date, where he was so ready to impress a woman. He felt relaxed around Ava, in an odd kind of I'm-not-going-to-marry-you way.

"Should I sing?" He winked.

"Please do."

But two seconds later, Sally was beside them, Ava's pink-and-yellow cupcake with a lit candle on it as Sally sang "Happy Birthday." She set the two cakes down and went back behind the counter to sulk.

"I think we woke her," Max said. "So, why a coffee shop? I'm not discouraging you, but I just want to know what led you."

"That's easy. I've had a love affair with coffee for years."

"So does ninety percent of the population but you don't see most of them opening up a business serving it."

"I guess it goes back to my nanny, Lucia. She practically raised me."

"Your mother didn't—"

"Take time off to raise us? No, but I don't blame her for that. She needed her career to keep her satisfied with life. And she found me the best substitute mom in the world."

"That's high praise."

He felt as if an anvil had been lifted from his chest. As Ava went on about the woman who'd raised her and her brothers, Max understood that at least one person had loved her without conditions. And apparently, that woman loved coffee enough to have shared the passion with Ava.

"It's the smell of coffee that I love most." She lowered the paper on one side of her cupcake. "That dark, rich, intense flavor when its brewed. It fills the kitchen with aroma. Reminds me of love."

Max devoured his cupcake in two bites. "And where is she now? Does she offer advice on coffee beans?"

"Of course, but I haven't seen her for a few years. She moved back to Colombia when I went to college. After college, I was able to take a year off and went to stay with her and her family. I've never had a better time. We ate, we danced, we had parties that sometimes lasted all night long. I even had a short love affair with a young coffee bean farmer." She tipped her head and sent him a sly smile.

He quirked a brow. "Should I be worried?"

"Yes, fake boyfriend, you should be *really* worried. We had a great love affair. I didn't speak much Spanish and he spoke no English, so we never talked. Possibly my most successful relationship to date."

That made him laugh. "How could you go wrong?"

"For all I know, he's still waiting for me to come back." She finally took a bite of cupcake and wound up wiping some frosting off her nose.

They were joking, all in good fun, so it made no sense that a ripple of jealousy spiked through him.

It was an unproductive emotion, not to mention non-sensical in his case, so he slammed it back.

"She sounds like my mother. My family has a large party for everyone's birthday, from the oldest family member to the youngest infant. Huge trays of arroz con pollo, dancing in the outdoor patio and, lord help me, karaoke."

"Oh, I love karaoke!" She clapped her hands.

"Why am I not surprised."

"Does your family ever ask you to sing?"

"Not if they prefer to live."

Her tongue flicked out to lick a bit of frosting from her pinky finger and he flashed on the memory of the time they'd kissed. It wasn't his custom to kiss a woman like that and then never talk about it again. But she hadn't brought it up, either. She'd challenged him, and that's the only reason he'd kissed her. To prove a point. The fact that he was thinking about kissing her again, well, that was another problem entirely.

"What I want to know," she said, fixating him with those clear emerald eyes. "Is what happened to *you*? You wanted to know how I wound up the way I am coming from the family that I did. Now you know. But it sounds like you should have been born into my family, and maybe I should have been born into yours."

Max struggled with how he could put into words something that might cause Ava to feel guilty. She'd lived a privileged life, and he hadn't. Not even close.

He wanted her to realize that because of that privilege the advantages afforded her were ones she'd maybe taken for granted.

But Ava wasn't like any of the other privileged people he'd met. She'd clearly walked away from all of it, including the pleasure of driving a superior car. He wasn't sure *he* could have done that. Her life in Charming was quiet, and unassuming, and clearly most people had little to no idea of where she'd come from and what she'd given up.

No. Ava was down-to-earth, honest and kind.

She reminded him of home.

"My first job was picking strawberries, right alongside my parents and younger sisters. Sure, it was a family activity too, because my parents tried to make it one. We all did it together, just like we lived. But the work was backbreaking. I promised myself that my children would never have to work that hard."

These days, he often relaxed by working in his backyard garden, a small connection to his past. It wasn't the hard work of the picking fields but for him, still steeped in memories of home, family, love.

"I'm sorry. I didn't know." She leaned forward and covered his hand with hers.

"Don't be sorry. It's made me appreciate everything I have much more. But along the way, I guess I got really serious about everything. Starting with my grades, of course. I wasn't satisfied with a B. My parents didn't push me. I pushed myself. I always wanted more. Better. The navy was my ticket to an education and from there I kept excelling. It got to where I couldn't stop. Like a drug."

Damn, it was the first time he'd admitted it to himself.

"I admire you for that. And I also admire your parents for supporting you, while not pushing you."

"To them, I always worked too hard, and took life way too seriously."

"Well, I'm with your family on this one. Sometimes you do take life too seriously."

"I don't want to fail at anything. Especially not marriage."

"I can understand that. Were you ever married before?"

"No, but I came pretty close a couple of times. It wouldn't have worked so I'm glad I didn't go through with it."

"And why wouldn't it have worked?" She cocked her head.

"Cheating."

"Yours or theirs?"

"Theirs, of course. Can you imagine me as a cheater?"

"No, I can't, you're far too serious for that. But I had to ask. After all, I know so little about my fake boyfriend."

"Cheating is a common problem in the navy. Some women don't like being left alone for long stretches of time."

"Then they shouldn't have signed up for that."

If only it had been that simple, but apparently there was something oddly attractive about a navy man. And also, something very forgettable.

"Right," he said, glancing at his wristwatch. "Whenever you're ready."

Max was being so *nice*. Ava hated that it probably had everything to do with pity, but tonight she'd take the sympathy. Rather than fix him up with Mercedes, she should have realized that one evening with her family might help him see what *his* future family might look like. She hoped he'd had second thoughts. Max was a good guy, who seemed to be hiding behind a false belief about himself.

After her cupcake, Ava fully expected him to drive her home, but instead he headed to the wharf. Saturday night was slammed at the Salty Dog.

"Did you want to stop by work?"

"I'm taking you to the boardwalk."

This was a side of Max she hadn't been familiar with and she wondered why he'd unwrapped it for her tonight. And how long it had been buried. Even though she actually relished the idea of going home to bed with a cup of coffee and a book, she'd be crazy to pass this opportunity up.

"I've never seen you on the boardwalk before."

"What do you mean? I've been there plenty of times."

"I don't mean when you walk across on the way to work, Max. I'm talking about the rides. The games."

"Okay, you got me. Never have. But this is your night and I bet you appreciate the carnival-like atmosphere."

"Is that a dig? Don't look now, but Mr. Grumpy is peeking his ugly head out."

"I'm not being a grump, I just thought you might like this, and I want to make you happy. Anything wrong with that?"

"Nope."

So, she didn't complain when he bought her cotton candy, even though she much preferred salty and sweet kettle corn from the Lazy Mazy. If they'd looked overdressed at the bakery, that went double for the wharf. Droves of residents and a few tourists crowded the boardwalk tonight, moving from games to rides dressed in jeans, board shorts and tees. Some of the younger children were already dressed in Halloween costumes. The weather tonight was classic with a light coastal breeze. Perfect and mild.

"Ava!" Barbara from the yarn store waved and approached. "Don't you look lovely."

"Hi, Barbara!" Ava went in for a hug.

"You're so dressed up. What's the occasion?"

"It's her birthday," Max volunteered.

"Oh, my goodness, I had no idea. Happy birthday."

"We went out to dinner with my family, which is why we're dressed up."

Barbara quirked a brow and Ava read the message loud and clear: *Are you dating* Max*?* Before she could return the silent message *no*, Barbara's kids appeared, each looking stickier than the other. One had on a Spider-Man costume, the other Batman.

"Ava! Look what I have," Joe Bob said, almost levitating. "I won it at the arcade!"

He proudly held up a plastic Frisbee and waved it around.

"Wow, that's awesome."

"Stop waving that around before you hurt your brother," Barbara said. "Max, did you know that largely because of Ava we had a huge turnout for our ribbon-cutting ceremony? It was in the middle of the day and I was worried that no one would come."

"That's our Ava," Max said, draping his arm around her shoulder.

"Oh, it was nothing." She shook her head and a blush crept up her neck at the unwelcome attention. "I just made a few calls."

"Bah, nothing. She even had the senior citizens come out to support us."

"Well, they like to knit." Ava held on to the sticky cotton candy. "And Susannah *is* my neighbor."

"I can never get her to come out," Barbara said. "She doesn't like to leave Doodle."

Joe Bob stared at Ava's cotton candy the way only a child could: with utter longing.

"Hey," Ava said. "Do you think the kids could have my cotton candy to share?"

Eyes bright and wide, both eyed Ava like she was Santa Claus.

"Okay," Barbara said with a quick nod. "They've been good tonight."

She handed the sticky sugar concoction to Barbara so she could dispense it.

"I'll see y'all soon," Barbara said, when one of her children tugged on her hand.

Max walked silently beside her for a few minutes, hands in the pockets of his pants. "You don't like cotton candy, do you?"

"They just seemed to want it more."

"I feel bad that I didn't get you anything for your birthday."

"Are you kidding? I talked you into this date."

He didn't say anything for a long beat. "But that's a fair exchange."

For a moment, she'd almost forgotten that she'd promised to find him his future wife, in exchange for this date and help with her business plan.

"You're right. Don't worry, I haven't forgotten our deal." She waited a beat. "But if you want to get me something for my birthday, I'm dying to go to the Bangles reunion concert next month."

"I'd rather be dragged through the desert and left for dead. Think of something else. Please." He stopped at a boardwalk game. "Here we go. I haven't done this kind of thing for years."

"Not this one," Ava whispered. "I think it's rigged."

One corner of his mouth tipped in a smile. "It probably is."

"Don't waste your money."

She wrapped her hand around his biceps to still him from moving forward, suddenly aware that she hadn't touched him tonight. Not since they left the restaurant holding hands for her family's benefit. She hadn't touched him like *this* since the night of their spontaneous kiss. The one he'd given her only to make a point. Not surprisingly, those biceps were still hard as a rock. She gulped.

"Don't worry. I'm not going to waste my money." He took out a few bills and handed them to the teen behind the booth. "It's all about the fun. Right?"

The game involved tossing nickels into jars that were strategically placed, exactly at points to make it unlikely for anyone but a sharpshooter to make. And though she was all about supporting business, someone had to be offering a product or service. This always felt more like a scam.

On the first round, Max tossed a nickel into every jar, shocking the clerk out of his daze.

"Great," he said without enthusiasm. "Go two more times and you get the grand prize, or stop now and pick from any of our prizes right over there."

"You should stop now. How can you be that lucky twice in a row?" Ava hissed.

Max went for it, making every jar two more times. Excitement bubbled up in Ava and she bounced, clapping and laughing every time he made the shot. This wasn't luck but pure skill.

"Wow. Just great." The clerk rolled his eyes. "You're awesome. Which grand prize do you want?"

He turned to Ava. "What's it going to be?"

There was no contest. Ava wanted the gorilla. When the clerk used a long stick to pull it down from the display, Max took the gorilla and handed it to Ava.

"I have to say, I didn't see it going that way," Max said as they continued to walk along the boardwalk.

"Thought I'd want the teddy bear?" She nuzzled the gorilla's fur. "I need my own eight-hundred-pound gorilla."

He blinked. "You never fail to surprise me."

She wobbled along, clutching her gorilla, wishing this night would never end. Her fake boyfriend was even better than the real thing. Suddenly, Max stopped, and his gaze slid down her legs to her feet.

"I'm an idiot. You're wearing high heels." He tugged her to a nearby bench. "Sit."

She didn't argue at the order because she desperately wanted to sit down. Not one to complain, she'd tried to ignore the pain in her feet. She should have slipped them off earlier, but she did now, taking both off, and rubbing the heels of her feet.

Before she knew it, Max took one of her feet and started rubbing. "You should have said something."

She swallowed hard, heart thudding in her ears, because the caress from his warm fingers felt sweet and delicious. Intimate. Though it clearly wasn't. Max was simply performing a duty and obligation. He'd walked her around until her feet ached, so now he would fix that.

"I should have, but I'm having too much fun."

Max opened his mouth, then shut it. His jaw visibly tightened. She followed his gaze and saw Nick, the Salty Dog's head chef, walking around with a gorgeous redhead on his arm.

"Is that Nick? Who's he with?"

Worry prickled her at Max's sudden intensity, and she thought that maybe Nick was with someone Max had once dated or been interested in. He might be jealous. Nick was a real player, a different woman every week, it seemed. He wasn't particularly handsome, but had an interesting face, and a very outgoing personality.

"She's pretty," Ava said.

"And very married."

"Wh-what?" Ava moved, which made Max's hand slip and wind up on her knee.

Oh, sweet thrill! "She's married? Are you sure?"

"Unfortunately."

Now Ava understood. Nick had offended Max's sensibilities and sense of right and wrong. And she kind of loved that about him. Nick passed by, his arm low on the woman's back, practically resting on her tiny rump. Though they were several feet away and could have easily been ignored, Max called out.

"Hey, Nick."

The voice was loud and forceful enough that Nick stopped to follow the sound. His animated face went from relaxed to someone who'd been caught with his hand in the proverbial cookie jar. Face drained of color, he walked over, letting go of the redhead quite suddenly, as if he could get rid of her that easily. No such luck, as she followed.

"Hey, how's it going, you two? Nice gorilla." He leaned back, feigning shock. "Are you two on a *date*?"

"It's Ava's birthday," Max said, tone dripping irritation.

"Oh hey, happy birthday there, Ava." When the redhead wouldn't go away, he finally threw his arm around her shoulders, friendship-style. "Sheryl and I are just hanging out."

"That's right. We're just good friends," Sheryl said with a saucy wink. "Hi, Max."

Max did not reply but simply nodded.

"Well, we best get going," Nick said. "Ava, drop by tomorrow and I'll make you a special birthday lunch."

"Um, thanks. I will." She waved as they walked away, then turned to Max. "Awkward."

"He's an idiot."

"I can't argue with that, but it does take two to tango, or line dance, or two-step. You catch my drift." She clutched the gorilla she'd just silently named Tarzan.

Max turned to her and the scowl that had been on

his face had slipped. There was the slightest tip at the corner of his mouth, and his eyes... Those beautiful eyes were smiling, crinkles on the sides.

She loved making him smile, even a tiny bit.

"Let me ask you something. As a business owner, will you be able to make the tough decisions? The ones no one else will make?"

She gnawed on her lower lip. "You mean firing someone, don't you?"

He nodded. "I get to be the hard-ass. Cole doesn't have the stomach for it."

"I suppose that I'll have to be ready for that." She waited a long beat, imagining how tough that might be. She couldn't possibly fire a single mother. "Are you going to fire Nick?"

"Yeah. Probably. It's not his personal life, because much as I hate it, who he dates is none of my business. But he's letting this cross into his professional life and I can't let that happen. I don't think he respects us enough. Maybe this is just a stop for him."

"Have you ever fired someone?"

"Yeah, many times, and I will tell you something—most people see it coming. They know when they're screwing up."

"I'm just going to have to do a stellar job of screening my baristas."

"That too." He stood and offered his hand. "Ready?"

She wasn't prepared for this night to be over because this was one of the best times she'd had in months. With the last man on earth she'd have thought would have the patience. Then again, it was her birthday, and he probably felt bad for her.

She slipped her shoes back on and when she looked up Max was scowling again. "What?"

He gave her his back. "Climb on."

"Climb on your… No, Max." She hesitated to tell him that she didn't want to be a *literal* burden. Besides, what if she weighed too much for his poor back?

"Do it. I'm carrying you back to the car."

"But I can walk."

"You mean limp, don't you? Climb me."

When he put it that way…his back looked strong enough to carry a beast of burden. Or something. She argued a bit more with him—useless, because she'd already learned that Max didn't back down when he wanted something. Seconds later, she was on his back, dress hiked up to her thighs, her arms wrapped around his broad shoulders, holding on to both him and Tarzan. They must have made quite a pair, because more than a few people smiled their way. Some openly stared.

A few minutes later they were at her home, and Ava struggled with whether she should ask him inside or not. This was not an actual date, but on a real date, there might be a kiss at the end. Max, ever the gentleman, led her to the front door.

Hand on her doorknob, she turned to him. "Do you want to come inside?"

A moment passed between them, and Ava felt the tension, thick as rich espresso. Max's warm gaze settled on her and in that moment, she felt he'd kiss her again. Not like the first time, when it had been to make a point. But now, he'd kiss her because he wanted to. She was dreaming, though, because she'd agreed to find him the perfect woman.

"I better go. I've got an early morning." A moment later, he tucked a stray hair behind her ear. "Sorry if I was a grump."

"What? No, I've had the best time tonight. Thank you, Max, not just for coming to dinner but for cupcakes, cotton candy, and…well, mostly for Tarzan." She held up the gorilla.

"You named him Tarzan?" He cocked his head and one corner of his amazing mouth curled up.

She laughed and beat Tarzan's hands on his chest. "I'll find a special place for him."

"You do that."

Chapter Nine

It was a good thing that Max had already made up his mind to fire Nick. Because if last night's display hadn't been enough to confirm his decision, the next morning, Nick showed up two hours late to work once again. Max had planned to wait until Adam arrived to let Nick go, but he couldn't tolerate the disrespect another minute.

"We need to talk." Max hooked his thumb to one of the booths.

"I'm already late. I have so much to do before we open."

"Sit."

Nick did, looking sheepish. "Look, I'm sorry. I had a little trouble this morning."

"Sheryl's husband again?"

"Why? Did he drop by here again?" Shifty-eyed Nick made good work of those eyes.

"No," Max said with patience. People were so damn stupid. It was like Nick had deliberately hopped on a train to Nowhere. "Not yet, anyway."

"Look, I know my head hasn't been in the game for a while."

Bingo. As Max always suspected, someone about to get canned knew they deserved it. They saw it coming.

"It's Sheryl. She won't leave me alone. I realize she's a married woman but dayum." He fanned his hand to indicate heat.

Max scowled. Nick, blaming his troubles on someone else. He couldn't take another minute of this shit show. "I'm going to have to let you go."

Nick returned the scowl. "Are you *kidding*? You're firing me? Is Cole okay with this?"

"Yep."

"I doubt that." He stood, fists clenched. "Cole is reasonable. He'll understand."

"I've given you plenty of chances. You only get two with me." Max stood as well, facing off.

Nick narrowed his eyes, but then his hands went up. "You know what? Forget this place! I can find better work *and* a better salary."

Max hadn't expected him to take this well, but the overt hostility surprised him. "Go for it."

"Ah, hell! You know what? You need to get laid!

You're a slave driver. All you do is work, and I'm tired of your crap." With that, he stalked toward the entrance, then turned back. "Send my last check. I don't want to step inside this crappy place again."

Max breathed a sigh of relief to be rid of the dead weight, even if he was now down one cook. Their most experienced cook. No matter. After checking the schedule, he noted they were unfortunately now down two cooks due to a previously scheduled day off for one of their staff. He'd have to fill in today. He rolled up his sleeves, went in the kitchen, washed his hands, and donned an apron. When Sam and Brian arrived for their shifts (early) Max was ready.

"What the hell?" Brian said, grabbing an apron. "Whatcha doin' boss?"

"Where's Nick?" Sam asked.

"Fired him."

"For real?" Brian said.

"He burned off my last nerve. I have a few part-timers that have asked for more hours. We'll do that until our new head cook arrives. Adam Cruz. You guys are going to love him. He's always on time and if he's not on time he's early."

"Can he cook?" Sam said.

Adam could do anything required of him, including single-handedly drag five men out of enemy territory. Unfortunately, Max happened to know that for the past several years he'd been shiftless, moving from one place to another. Cook had been just one of his many temporary jobs.

A few hours later, Max had been well schooled in the art of the fry cook. This definitely wasn't as easy as it looked. He'd mix drinks any day before he'd slave over a hot, greasy stove. But he was stuck now. His own damn fault. Should have asked Adam sooner. Max began to wonder if he was more of a hindrance than a help back here. He was trying. Flipping burgers and burning steaks.

And working his ass off. They still worked with an old-fashioned system from the previous owner, and that would be the next thing Max would change in the kitchen. As soon as he got a chance, he would install a monitor, and they'd go to a digital order system. They might be a historical landmark but that didn't mean they had to do everything the old-fashioned way. The archaic way of reading the slips of paper put on a carousel might be quaint but it wasn't efficient.

Valerie hung a slip of paper on the carousel and spun it. "What did Nick do now?"

"Oh, crap." Debbie, their oldest waitress, came up beside Valerie. "Sheryl's husband again?"

"No," Max said, "But we won't have to deal with him anymore."

He didn't encourage further talk and they both got the message. Never put Max in a hot kitchen and expect him to chat. And all of a sudden, as if something in the universe snapped, insanity broke loose. Valerie and the other waitresses were putting up orders it seemed every second. The carousel was filled.

"What the hell is going on?" Max said. "Is there a convention in town?"

Brian stared at him as if he was a simpleton. "Lunch rush."

"Right."

For the first time in his life, Max felt like a slug. No matter how fast he ran from one side of the kitchen to the other, from the fridge to the microwave to the stove Brian and Sam ran circles around him. They flipped burgers and plated dishes. These guys were all getting a raise as soon as he went over the books.

"Max," Valerie called out over the loud din of sizzling burgers and clanging pans. "Ava's here and she said that yesterday Nick offered her a birthday lunch special. Want me to tell her?"

Damn! Ava's lunch special. "Never mind, I'll take care of it. What does she usually have?"

"A turkey burger on whole wheat, hold the mayo. No special sauce. Lettuce, no onion, no pickle, sliced tomato. And sweet potato fries, just make sure they're crispy."

Max blinked. "Why don't you write that down for me."

"I've got it, boss." Brian had already pulled a turkey burger from the freezer and slapped it on the grill. "She's a picky one. Gotta get it right, too, because she won't send it back."

Score one more thing he'd discovered about Ava. Last night, he'd learned a lot about this woman who constantly surprised him. She'd been raised by her nanny, who seemed to have exerted the biggest influence on her life. Spent a gap year in Colombia, had an affair with a coffee farmer. Despite the fact that she was almost constantly cheerful, she had a morose side to her. A quiet and introspective side when someone had hurt her. Surprisingly, he kind of hated it.

And she was gorgeous. So beautiful, wearing a tiara on her head and pulling it off without looking the slightest bit ridiculous. A blond Audrey Hepburn, playing in *Sabrina*, of course. And the 800-pound gorilla. Safe to say he hadn't smiled that much in a year or more.

Brian shoulder checked Max as he plated the burger and fries. "Order up."

He must be getting old. These guys made him feel like he was standing still.

Like no matter how fast he moved, he couldn't keep up.

Valerie set Ava's turkey burger down. "Gossip!"

"What happened?" Ava leaned forward.

"Nick? He was fired this morning."

"Max said he was doing that, but I had no idea it would be *today*."

"I'm not even sure Max did, because we're short a cook now. And guess who's in the kitchen all sweaty, gorgeous, and rockin' an apron?"

Ava scrunched up her nose. The bar section was

closed but they sometimes didn't open for lunch on weekdays. "Cole?"

"Max."

Max. She'd give anything to see this. Valerie was off to her next customer, while Ava picked at her turkey burger and fries. He'd obviously made the tough decision. The one he'd warned her about. A business owner couldn't get sentimental about their employees. They sometimes had to make the tough choices no one else could. She'd listened carefully to his warning. It sometimes held her back, the knowledge that she'd control everything, and make judgments affecting real people. Real people who had mortgages and car payments. She'd make decisions that would affect a family's livelihood. It was both thrilling and frightening. And such a huge responsibility that she sometimes felt more comfortable just staying in her own little corner.

Oh dear. That might be the first time she'd admitted this to herself.

A few minutes later, Ava was halfway done with her lunch when her phone rang, and she fished it out of her purse. Caller ID read *Charming Hall*, the venue Ava had selected for the mayor's anniversary party. It was the only place reasonably priced to fit in the large crowd expected.

"I've got some bad news," Camilla said. "We somehow double booked the hall. I'm afraid we can't accommodate the mayor's party."

"The party is next Friday!"

"I know and I'm really so sorry."

"And you just noticed now? Why can't you bump the *other* party?"

"It's a wedding, hon, and you know how brides can be. I don't want that kind of bad ju-ju. If I cancel a week before the wedding, there will be blood and intestines on the floor of the hall. With you, I know you'll just find another place lickety-split."

How nice. She supposed this is what Ava got for being so easygoing and good-natured.

I don't think this is fair. You suck.

Do you know how hard it's going to be to find someplace else now? And Tippi left me in charge!

These were all on Ava's tongue, but she also understood Camilla's position. She was a nice lady, a grandma-type that always called Ava when she had an unexpected opening just to see if she'd like to have first crack at the date. And Ava sure didn't want a bride scrambling at the last minute. One was a marriage, the other an elected official's party.

"Yeah. Okay," Ava said. "I'll find another place. Any leads are appreciated."

"Nothing now, but I'll keep you posted. How do you feel about having it in Galveston?"

"Let's see. How do I feel about having the *Charming* mayor's party in Galveston?" Ava took a deep breath. "I'd rather give up coffee for a year."

"Enough said."

Ava hung up and spent a few minutes on her phone scouting for other locations. But of course, she'd scoped those out months ago and by now it would be too late. Still, it was worth a few calls. She had a slow afternoon, and planned to use the lull to do her homework for class this week. Instead she'd get back to the office and start calling people. Ava looked for Valerie so she could say a quick goodbye and found that in the past few minutes all hell had broken loose.

"Valerie, I've been waitin' here for twenty minutes!" One of their regulars called out.

"Me too!" said another. "What's goin' on here?"

"Sorry, y'all, we're short a cook and doin' our best," Valerie said, flitting by Ava's booth and setting down an order of nachos nearby.

"What's going on?" Ava said, following her.

"We had to send Sam on a break and we're havin' a hard time in the kitchen," Valerie whispered. "Max is in a mood to end all moods. I bet he's regrettin' firing Nick today and that says something."

Poor Max. Despite what he wanted her to believe, she thought he might secretly hate having to let someone go. There was something deep inside him that still remembered the tough times. He'd just somehow learned to push sympathy and compassion aside and be all business. Something Ava would need to learn. If she wanted to be a success, she'd have to learn to assert herself and stop being so darn... well, nice.

Welp. She could make those phone calls later. Now, a friend needed her help. Ava moved swiftly behind the bar and tucked her purse out of sight. She rolled up her sleeves and headed to the kitchen, walking through the swinging doors. Nearly as fast as the Road Runner, Brian moved like the wind. So did Max, for that matter. But Max. Oh, sigh. Valerie had been right. Dayum but an apron agreed with him. His back to her, it rather nicely framed a perfect male butt.

"What?" he grunted.

Brian looked up first, just a flash of a glance in between moving like a ninja from microwave to stove to ovens. "Oh, hey, Ava."

Max turned to her, brow quirked. "What are *you* doing back here?"

He indeed looked sweaty. And hot. Double meaning there. "Um, I heard you're short a cook."

"We've got it handled," Brian said, moving swiftly, and she wouldn't be surprised if any moment now he started juggling plates.

"You're supposed to go on your break," Max ordered. "Now, Brian."

"I'm just supposed to leave you two amateurs back here?"

"You have to," Max said. "It's the law. And Sam will be back soon. Go. I can handle this."

"No, you can't." Brian removed his apron and saluted. "But what the heck. Here, Ava. Do your best."

Ava tied the apron on which was at least two sizes too big for her. Max turned to her in between working on an iron skillet. "You get out of here too. I'll be fine."

"I can't go. I'm not leaving you. You've got an unruly and hungry crowd out there. You don't want a mob."

"They can always go *home* and eat if they want faster service. Or drive through the Golden Arches."

"I know you don't mean that, seeing as that might slowly put you out of business." She rubbed her hands together and wondered what she should do first.

Washing her hands seemed like a great first step.

Valerie and Debbie were grabbing plates from under the heating lamp so quickly it was soon empty. Best get to working on another order. She picked one off the carousel. Fortunately, this looked like Valerie's clear and neat handwriting.

"Easy. This is just an order of sweet potato fries."

"I mean it. Get out of here. I don't have time to argue with you," Max said.

"I'm not going to leave a friend high and dry. You need me, Max. It's okay that you can't admit it."

Ava looked for the bag of frozen fries in the freezer and the refrigerator. No dice. Meanwhile, Max had finished the skillet platter and was working on a steak.

"Um, Max? Hmm. I can't find the sweet potato fries in the freezer."

Hand on her back, he steered her to a plastic covered container of freshly cut sweet potato fries in the refrigerator.

"Oh, nice. Gosh, no wonder they always taste so good." She found the fry basket and stuck some in, then lowered it until she heard the sizzle. "Okay. That's done."

"I don't have insurance to cover you back here." Max took another slip of paper from the carousel. "Get out."

"Don't worry, I won't sue."

"Ava, damn it."

"This is all my fault. I blame myself."

"How's that?" He had time to quirk a brow before he set the steak on a plate, then headed for the salad fixings.

"If not for you trying to cheer me up, we wouldn't have been on the boardwalk last night. You wouldn't have seen Nick and that woman. Last night I should have talked you into giving Nick another chance. Then you wouldn't be in this position."

"I regret nothing."

"Maybe you shouldn't reject my help then." She went hands on hips.

"Ava!" He came around her so fast that he nearly knocked her down. "You forgot to flip the timer. These are ready."

Oh lord of the fries! They were indeed ready. "Sorry. I won't do that again."

With what she imagined to be great restraint, Max didn't bite her head off. "That's okay. It took me a few hours to get into the swing of this."

"You've been here all morning? When do *you* get a break?"

"The boss doesn't get a break."

"The hell he doesn't. You're not superhuman, mister. You're just not."

"I'll get my break when the second shift comes in."

Valerie took another plate from the heating lamp. "I called Cole, and I don't want to hear another word about it!"

"You didn't call *Cole*?" Ava yelled.

"It's his day off," Max muttered, chopping an onion. Hacking, more like it.

She stilled his hand. He looked about to chop a finger off. "Let me do this, at least."

They worked together, finally finding a silent and easy groove. Ava would reach for the ticket and call the order out to Max, then start working on the part of the order that didn't involve heat. Max had commandeered the fryer and grill and wouldn't let her near it again, once quirking a brow while simultaneously brandishing a large kitchen knife. She got the message, and stuck to the microwave, and pulling out the pre-cut vegetables, and pre-made soups.

And she found she really did her best when it was time for clean plates from the industrial dishwasher.

Chapter Ten

Shortly after Sam and Brian returned, a wonderful thing happened. The lunch rush ended. People went *home*. Most of them, anyway. A few came in here and there, but it was nothing like the two-hour-long Armageddon he'd just lived through. And Max found that he'd enjoyed working next to Ava, even if she'd behaved like the single most stubborn woman on the planet. She'd refused to leave, planting her feet like a tree. But once they'd found a groove and he'd kept her away from the fryer, it wasn't half bad.

Kind of nice, actually, to have a friend jump in and assist. She'd helped with something that had to have been uncomfortable for her, and new. Her support had been…unexpected. Kind. Within minutes,

they'd fallen into a smooth rhythm of working together that reminded him of the old days working
alongside his family in the fields. There, every link
in the chain contributed. Mattered. No matter how
hard or demeaning the work. He didn't believe he'd
missed that, but experiencing it again with Ava, with
Brian, Sam and later Cole, the memories weren't
horrible. After all, hard physical work was an honorable thing.

"Next time call me sooner," Cole said, taking a
pull of his beer.

After the second shift arrived, Cole, Valerie, Max
and Ava had gathered at a booth to recover. Cole and
Valerie, of course, were sitting on one side practically in each other's laps. Max sat next to Ava, who
was cradling her coffee mug.

The dinner "rush" didn't seem nearly as intense
but maybe it never looked that way from this side.
Still, at the moment the sounds of couples talking,
laughing, their silverware tinkling, was simply a soft
lull in the background.

"I haven't worked this hard in years," Max said.
"It's humbling."

He'd once heard a professor say that the more
education acquired, the less need to work with their
hands. And it wasn't shame that led Max away from
manual labor, but just the persistent belief that he had
to do better. Be better. If he still liked to work with
his hands, and he did, now it was simply a hobby.

"It feels good, though, doesn't it?" Valerie said.

"Sometimes after a hard day I just feel like I've pushed this body as far as it will go. And it's gratifying on some level. Of course, I wouldn't want to do it every day. That's why I'm a teacher."

"As if that's not hard?" Ava quipped from next to Max.

"A different kind." Valerie smiled and gazed at Cole, who took on that lovesick, gobsmacked look Max had seen on him for months.

Cole seemed a bit stunned some days, as if surprised he'd bagged a woman like Valerie, and about as happy as Max had ever seen him. It brought Max's thoughts back to his own plans for a serious and committed relationship. He had no idea what it might be like to feel so smug and self-assured when it came to a woman. No idea what it might feel like to love someone so much you'd be willing to take them warts and all.

Speaking of which, none of these dating services mentioned anyone's flaws. He supposed that was something for couples to find out as they dated and got to know each other. The whole idea had started to overwhelm him and he considered backing out. As far as he knew, Ava still had plans to find him the perfect wife. Clearly, she didn't consider herself in the running. Then again, she'd seen his list. She didn't know he'd purposely written in some stricter requirements that would exclude her. He thought it would be easier that way.

Not so much now.

He'd started to regret that ridiculous list now. Besides, it had been meant to simply be a guideline. Surely, she'd see that eventually.

"Well, guys, I should go," Ava said. "I've got a lot of phone calls to make. And while I have you here, if you'd planned to attend the mayor's party next week, the location has changed."

"Where is it now?" Max had planned to attend, of course, and rub elbows with any and all of the influential.

"I'll let you know."

"I thought it was at the hall," Valerie said.

"They double-booked us, and obviously the wedding is more important," Ava said.

Funny, she didn't appear to believe this.

"I hope you gave 'em hell," Max said.

"Oh, yeah. Sure, I did." She cleared her throat. "But now I have to find a new venue."

Valerie leaned forward. "The answer is pretty obvious to me."

"It is?" Ava scrunched up her nose.

She was kind of adorable, actually.

"Tippi owns the lighthouse," Valerie said, turning to Cole. "We should have it there."

"Oh, no, Tippi would never ask that of you. You pay rent there and she respects your privacy."

"We're offering," Valerie said. "Right, baby?"

"Sure, I don't mind." Cole slung an arm over Valerie and pulled her in even closer. "It's her house."

"Well… I suppose there might be a way," Ava said, chewing on her bottom lip.

Her wheels were spinning, and damn it was a beautiful site.

"We could set up an area outside on the beach," Valerie said.

"A tent, maybe. Some fairy lights," Ava added.

"People could just spill in and out of the lighthouse," Valerie said. "Plenty of standing room."

And they were off.

It wasn't all that surprising that these two had become such fast friends, even if Ava had had a not-so-secret crush on Cole for a while. They hadn't dated, but once Valerie showed up that was all she wrote. Cole hadn't so much as looked at another woman.

Max stared at Cole, who seemed equally uninterested in the party planning. Max nudged his chin to the back office and rose. Cole unwrapped himself from Valerie and followed. When Max opened the door, Sub immediately rose from his dog bed and came to him, wagging his tail. He dispensed pats and rubs, then took a seat on the office chair behind the desk.

"Something wrong?" Cole asked as he rummaged behind the desk and pulled out a small flask.

"Not at all. I was thinking. After today, I'd like to sweeten the pot for Adam." He stretched his legs. "We're talking about a decorated leader, Cole. Someone we both owe our lives to. I don't see him lasting long in that kitchen unless he has a vested interest. Let's bring him in."

"As a partner?" Cole set two shot glasses on the desk.

"Absolutely. If he can afford to buy in, and if he's interested, let's do it. We can give up some equity and the influx of additional cash will be what we need to up our game."

"You want to install the digital ordering system, don't you?" Cole smirked.

"Among many other improvements that will simply make life easier for everyone."

"If the Historical Society allows us." Cole poured two shots from the flask.

"Right."

"Off the subject," Cole said, "but I was also thinking—did you ever consider that maybe you can't just approach this 'looking for a wife' thing like you do a mission?"

"A mission?" Max squinted. What in the hell was Cole talking about? "I haven't planned a mission in years."

"I disagree." Cole slammed back his shot glass. "Why do you want to get married?"

"It's time and I'm ready."

Now Cole squinted at Max. "You know it doesn't work that way."

"Yeah." Max sighed. "I'm beginning to realize that."

"I want you to think about why all of a sudden it

became the right time. And don't give me all that rot about retirement plans and savings. You and I both know this bar could go belly-up at any time. We're doing well now, but…"

Max stomach clenched and he slammed back his own shot. Buying into the bar was the greatest financial risk he'd ever taken, but he'd have done anything for Cole.

"Are you *trying* to give me heartburn?"

"It's the right time because you met the right woman. She's right in front of you every single day. And I've seen the way you look at her."

Max didn't have to ask who Cole meant. It was the bright and shiny light of a woman who everyone loved on some level. Ms. Sunshine.

"She's not interested."

"Are you sure about that?"

Max wasn't sure of anything. If felt like his world had gone off rotation. If this had been a mission, it would have been declared a disaster. Retreat! Surrender. Aw, hell no. Max Del Toro did not give up on anything, or anyone.

"I'm pretty damn sure she is," Cole said with a smile. "But it's you who's going to have to take the risk and find out."

In the end, the toughest thing about moving the celebration to the lighthouse was informing all their guests of their new location. Ava made the calls, which took roughly half a day. Tippi had only been slightly upset to hear of the double-booking fiasco, but when Ava had been able to segue into their new location, she was appeased. She would have never asked to impose on Cole but appreciated the idea.

With Valerie's helpful event-planning experience, Ava was looking forward to another successful Charming event.

The hardest part she'd have to do in the next few minutes. But it was time.

A man as wonderful as Max deserved the best and Ava would not fail him this time. Darcie Abbott had graduated from Princeton, too. With a similar upbringing to Ava's, she hadn't turned her back on her family legacy. Darcie worked in civil law at the family firm of Abbott & Abbott. She worked for high-profile clients but her own kindness and compassion for the less fortunate had her giving her time to several pro bono organizations. Tall and willowy, she was educated, intelligent, brunette and within Max's "age requirements."

She'd done what she promised to do, but Ava's stomach had been a quivering mess since the day she'd called Darcie and invited her to a party where she'd meet a very special man. Luckily, or maybe not so luckily, Darcie had just ended an engagement to a fellow attorney who'd argued with her on the definition of "fidelity." Apparently, he thought he'd won in closing arguments. He had not. Darcie swore then that she'd never date another lawyer. Enter Max. He would be perfect for Darcie. The thought filled Ava with an ache she didn't understand.

She picked up her phone and texted Max.

I thought the mayor's party could serve double duty. Get ready to meet the most wonderful woman I know. If you don't like her, there's no hope for you and I give up. Her name is Darcie Abbott, she graduated from Princeton, and she'll be at the party.

She waited as the three little dots showed a message was coming. It took longer than she would have expected it to, seeing as it was a one-word reply: Okay.

"Okay? That's all you have to tell me? *Okay?*"

Not: *Let's think about this. What's she like? Did you check the list? I changed my mind. I have a new list and guess what, she doesn't have to be brunette. Let's forget the whole thing.*

She threw her phone down on the couch, where it landed next to Sub, who was resting comfortably and didn't move a muscle.

"Is that all who has to tell you?"

Valerie appeared at the foot of the winding staircase holding a box.

The lighthouse was one of Ava's favorite places in Charming and if Cole and Valerie ever gave up the lease, she'd move right in. There were portholes for windows, and sunbeams left random patches of light. The windows gave a breathtakingly beautiful view of the Gulf. The floors, a teakwood, gleamed.

"Oh, just… Max." Ava really needed to get a grip. "I told him I found him the perfect woman and he said…he said 'okay.'"

"Such enthusiasm." Valerie carried the box to the coffee table made out of one long slab of wood. "And who in the world believes he can have the perfect woman?"

"I don't know. The perfect man?"

While she thought his idea of a list was stupid, and offensive, she now knew a lot more about the man and understood why he felt as if he always had to prove his worth. Why he'd always worked so hard, and mistakenly decided that he could do the same when it came to the search for a real partner.

Her heart twisted each time she thought of little Max in the fields. Helping his family. Maybe going hungry some nights. Someone who came from that kind of a struggle would never want to go back to it. She didn't understand…but she could imagine. When she'd been to Colombia, she'd seen real poverty, but Nanny Lucia did all right, largely thanks to how generous Ava's parents had been. Still, it had humbled her to know how easy she'd had it when others in the world struggled so much.

"Max is many things, but perfect is not one of them." Valerie opened the box of fairy lights they would be stringing outside to decorate. "And can I see this list?"

Ava picked up her phone, pulled up the text and showed it to Valerie.

"Wow. Is this a *joke*?"

Ava shook her head. "Note how nearly every requirement is the opposite of me."

"And you care. Why?"

"Sure. I mean, of course. In a perfect world, you know…well." She waved her hand dismissively. "Never mind."

"No. Tell me."

"I just… I have strong feelings for him, that's all. He's…not who I thought."

Valerie took Ava's hands in hers. "Oh my gosh, Ava. Just tell him how you feel."

"What for? We've spent some time together. The birthday dinner date was…really nice. He got me a cupcake, and we went to the boardwalk afterward. But if he'd wanted me to stop looking for his perfect wife, he would have told me by now. He hasn't. Instead, when I told him about Darcie, he said 'okay.'"

"Cheer up. Maybe she won't like him."

Ava snorted. "No, she's going to love him. They're perfect for each other."

"I'm really getting sick of hearing all this 'perfect' stuff. There's no such thing as two people who are perfect for each other. There are always going to be differences. People are inherently flawed, just as they should be. You find love when there's a real connection. When you see something in each other that no one else can. When you need each other because you bring out the best in each other. And some-times two very different people can find that, too."

"It's too late. I already gave up."

"Look, whether or not he likes this woman, whether or not she's perfect for him, you should tell him how you feel. You never know. He could sur-prise you."

But he already had. He was kinder than she'd imagined and asked questions that pushed her to think in different ways about old subjects. And he clearly had her back.

"There's nothing I can do about it now. She's com-ing, and she'll either hate him or love him. I think my future is in her hands." She shrugged. "At least she's a good person."

"You are forgetting one tiny detail." Valerie hooked an arm around Ava's shoulder. "*He* might not want *her*."

But Ava didn't think so. No, not in a million years. There was a reason she'd waited to phone Darcie.

Because she was exactly what Max wanted, and the knowledge of that slid into Ava's heart with a solid punch.

Chapter Eleven

Well, damn. It had been a week since Max had taken Ava to the family birthday dinner. A week since she'd been such a great help to him in the kitchen. During the week, they'd talked when they ran into each other at the bar or texted on days when they didn't. Mostly they'd talked about her business plan, which he'd reviewed, and made some changes to. He had plenty of ideas.

Max had begun to feel something he'd have never imagined slowly growing inside him. He'd never felt this comfortable and relaxed with a beautiful woman. He could be himself around Ava. Grumpy at times, he was certain annoying and anal at others, and still she seemed to like him. Then again, she *did* pretty much like everybody, and he shouldn't have felt special.

Now this.

She'd set him up with a woman.

The whole thing was your idea, genius.

He supposed he could blame this all on himself since he'd never told her to stop looking for his so-called perfect wife. When he'd never given her any indication that he was interested in her. Clearly, he'd received mixed signals from Ava on the night of her birthday dinner. The night when they'd walked along the boardwalk like a couple of teenagers. The night he'd nearly kissed her again and swore he'd seen that same invitation in her eyes. Wrong.

On the night of the stupid party, Max showered and dressed casual. Jeans, button-down shirt, didn't bother shaving. Take it or leave it, Donna Abbott, or whatever her name was. He didn't care anymore. He was a professional businessman, highly successful, and so what if he was a little clueless about love? It wasn't as if he'd had all kinds of time to devote to the study of it. He'd bet he wasn't the only former military man sick of the temporary stuff that only lasted until a woman found out he wasn't made out of steel. Until a woman realized the hard way that sometimes a military man carried a little extra baggage.

He'd been watching Sub all day so that Cole, Valerie and Ava could have zero distractions while they set up for this party. He and Sub had been surfing in the morning, and then hung out in front of the plasma TV screen watching football. Max alternately pitched popcorn for Sub to catch midair, and also threw it at the screen because of the quarterback's disgusting passes.

"C'mon, let's go, boy. It's that time. No more avoiding it."

He drove to the lighthouse with the top down, Sub in the front seat, buckled in of course. Valerie would kill him otherwise.

"Yap! Yark!" Sub pronounced louder the closer they got to the lighthouse.

"Yeah, yeah." He pulled into a spot behind Cole's truck and opened the door for Sub, who bounded toward the front door.

So, *he* was certainly excited about tonight. Max figured he should be, too. Maybe he should check his pulse. But he smelled the salty scent of the coast, heard the sound of the waves crashing, and he was clearly breathing, so he had to be alive. Cole threw open the door and Sub bounded into his arms like they'd been separated for years, not hours.

Maybe Max should get a dog.

"Hey, buddy. Who's a good boy?" Cole rolled on the ground with Sub, letting him have his fill of licks.

"You two should get a room already."

No sooner were the words out than Ava joined them, giving him an assessing look. "Hi, Max."

"Hey." He pretended his heart wasn't halfway in the gutter and that he'd arrived with every plan to steal Debbie's heart tonight. Or was it Dori?

"Hope this is acceptable. Sorry. No suit tonight."

"You look fine," she said, with a small smile.

"Yeah, leave the suit wearing to the others," Cole said.

Cole was dressed in his ever-present board shorts and a short-sleeved button-up, completely unbuttoned. Every bit the surfer dude he'd been for much of his life.

Valerie appeared in the doorway that led outside. "Baby, I could use your help out here. Oh hi, Max."

"Be right back," Cole said, and off he went to follow Valerie and do her heart's desire. Sub followed Cole, willing to do his master's desire, whatever that might be.

Max should definitely get a dog.

"The mayor and her staff will be here shortly," Ava said.

She'd moved into the kitchen where she was filling buckets with ice and stuffing soda and beer bottles inside of them.

"Here, let me help."

They worked side by side in silence. He noted that he'd only seen Ava this quiet and subdued after her family dinner. At least she wore colors: a short green dress, red sandals and a matching scarf. He wanted to remind her it wasn't Christmas yet, and two weeks ago he might have done just that.

But he hadn't ever met anyone who could wear so many colors at once and pull it off.

It felt good to be this near her, working in close

proximity. Her delicious flowery scent rose up to tease him. He knew from the night he'd kissed her that the perfume was in her hair, and he'd happily bury his nose there and die a happy man.

But first, meeting the woman of his dreams. Right.

"I think you'll really like Darcie," she said after several quiet minutes.

Darcie. Not Donna, or Debbie.

Remember that, brainless. "I'm sure I will."

"She should be here soon. Any minute now."

"Okay."

"Yes, that's what you keep saying. *Okay.*" She suddenly turned to him, green eyes flashing. "Try not to sound so darned enthusiastic!"

"I don't know what you want from me. Should I sing? Clap my hands in joy? Do a soft-shoe? Ava, you *know* me. I'm not easily excited."

"Maybe you should try a little, for the sake of Darcie. I've rolled out the best woman I could find for you, and the least you could do is get a little happy about it!"

"Sure. I'm happy."

"Oh my gosh, how can you *tell*?"

He scowled. "Take my word for it, will you?"

"Great, because I've worked really *hard* for you. I want to find the woman of your dreams!" With that, she viciously stuck a can of soda pop in the bucket and made a sound between a growl and a groan.

"Here, let me take these outside for you before you hurt them."

Right now, he needed a break from the woman currently playing hockey with his brain.

No sooner had Max carried the buckets of ice filled with drinks outside than Darcie Abbott was at the front door, looking like a runway model. She wore a classic black pantsuit, cinched in at the waist to showcase her amazing slender figure. Her dark hair had been styled in a pixie cut and looked incredibly soft and feminine as only she could pull off.

"Honey," Darcie said, opening her arms up for Ava. She had to bend down a little to reach her. "It's been way too long."

Ava ushered her inside. "Did you enjoy the drive?"

"When you emailed that you'd moved to Charming, I had no idea what to expect. No wonder you want to stay here. It's bucolic. Wonderful. I want to ask my dad to open up a satellite office down here. Hey, I could work at the beach. Right?"

"Sure. You'd love it here." Ava swallowed past the lump in her throat. It had tightened like a vise.

"Where is this magical woodland creature you've talked to me so much about?"

Ava walked Darcie to the porthole window that faced the beach. There was Max, involved in a conversation with Cole. He looked so handsome tonight that her ovaries had quivered at the sight of him. She wished he'd have given her some clue as to what he was thinking, but no, simply those deep hooded brown eyes that showed little to no emotion. He'd demonstrated more excitement the night he'd won Tarzan. She couldn't figure him out at all. One minute he showed her who he was, the next he was shut up tight again. Well, after tonight he'd be a mystery for Darcie to unravel.

Oh dear. There went that tug at her heart again. But Darcie was a good person and she deserved someone wonderful.

"Holy guacamole, that's one good-looking hunk of a man."

"The one with the dark hair, not the sandy blond who's just now leaning down to pet the cute dog."

"Yes, you said—tall, dark and handsome. Sister, you nailed it."

"Here, let's go introduce you. He can't wait to meet you."

But honestly, Ava wasn't so sure about that. He'd given her no more emotion about tonight than when he'd picked up his membership packet at the Chamber the first time they'd met. As if performing a duty expected of him. Sign up and be a part of the business community. It's the right thing to do.

Ava led Darcie outside through the living room sliders and down the steps to the area decorated tonight with folding chairs, chaise lounges and small folding tables. The caterers had set up the buffet of Tex-Mex food indoors, but some guests would be

seated outdoors under the moonlight and strategically placed lamplights.

The mild waves rolled in and out with their almost hypnotic rhythm. There was a light and lovely
breeze in the air that ruffled Ava's hair and the skirt
of her dress. Self-consciously, she snagged it down.
No need to give everyone a show. She should have
worn a classy pantsuit like Darcie, but Ava wasn't a
big fan of understated black.

Max and Cole noticed them coming and angled
their bodies toward them as they approached. Both
wore welcoming smiles. Cole's, of course, far more
open and genuine than Max's, which was simply a
slight curve of his lips.

"Gentlemen, this is my good friend, Darcie Abbott. Darcie, meet Cole Kinsella, and this…is Max
Del Toro."

Ava didn't know if it was her imagination, or if
Max's gaze really did linger on Ava before taking
Darcie's hand. "Nice to finally meet you."

Five whole words! "I better get back to the party.
The mayor will be here any minute now."

She rushed back up to the house without looking
back once. A few minutes later the mayor arrived,
her husband in tow, and the evening began. Lots of
hand shaking and gratitude from the mayor for her
supporters. Cocktails and dinner were served. As the
evening progressed, Ava made a point to lose track of
Max and Darcie. She'd seen them briefly in the room
when everyone had gathered at the buffet, standing

side by side in line. After that, she saw them outside laughing as they walked along the shore.

They were getting along, as she'd suspected. So, goodbye to anything more than friendship with Max.

You're a darn coward.

Whenever she'd cross eyes with Valerie, Ava noticed a look of sympathy that she didn't appreciate. She was going to be just fine, thanks! A small area in the living room had been cleared after the buffet, the regular furniture moved for the day.

"Let's have a little dancing, folks!" Ava called out and hit Play on her selected playlist.

When "Celebrate" piped through the speakers, Tippi and her husband took to the floor with others. Valerie and Cole joined in, Sub having been relegated to their bedroom upstairs once the food had been put out.

"Ava." She turned to find Darcie behind her, smiling. "We're going to be getting out of here in a few minutes."

"Oh, um, great. It's going well, huh?"

"*So* good. He's wonderful and I don't feel like we can really go deeper in getting to know each other while we're here, if you know what I mean?" She winked. "He seems kind of shy. I mean, I'm coming on pretty strong, and he hasn't even touched me."

Ava ignored the tiny flash of hope that burned like an ember. No need for that. Max was simply being a gentleman. Taking it *slow* with his future wife. Ava's heart wrenched and rattled painfully. Somehow, she'd foolishly started falling in love with this man.

"I'm going to suggest to him that we get out of here, and I just wanted you to know. And thank you, of course." She hugged Ava. "We'll catch up later and I'll give you all the saucy details."

"Oh, no, no, that won't be necessary."

Darcie winked again and with a little finger wave, she went back outside again, presumably to grab Max. To make herself feel better, Ava remembered all the pro bono work Darcie had done over the years. Because of her, people who couldn't afford quality representation got a chance in the legal system.

Ava wandered through the party, watching couples dancing, and Valerie and Cole cuddling on the couch like there was no one else in the room. She had her head on his shoulder, he was playing with her hair, and it was just so sweet and loving that Ava's heart tugged. She wanted to love someone like that.

"Ava, come on!" Tippi called out, doing the jig with her husband. "Join us, sugar! I've got my dancin' feet on tonight."

Oh, yeah. That's right. This was a party. She'd worn green and red, after all, which always lifted her spirits, anytime of the year. Ava joined everyone on the dance floor, doing what she did best. Faking happiness until she eventually forgot why she'd been hurting. Until she buried it with all the other memories. That time her mom had been at a medical conference and Daddy forgot to attend her dance recital when she'd had a solo. But he'd been wrapped up with a dying patient, so that was understandable. His work was life-and-death, and dance was just… something fun.

But Nanny Lucia had been in the audience, clapping and smiling widely.

When I was a younger woman I danced on tables, drank tequila and dated handsome men.

Well, Ava didn't have the handsome man, nor was she fond of tequila, but she had a table handy. As the throwback "We Are Family" anthem by Sister Sledge boomed through the speakers, Ava tugged off her sandals and jumped on the coffee table. She motioned for Tippi to join her, which she did. Next, Valerie wrenched herself out of Cole's arms and joined in.

Arms around her friends, Ava danced. And pretty soon faking the happy almost became real.

Chapter Twelve

"You sure know how to throw a party," one of the council members said, shaking Ava's hand.

"Anything for Tippi."

Equally grateful, Tippi and her husband had left a few minutes ago, but the party was still in full swing, others no doubt enjoying the ambience of the quaint lighthouse.

Ava glanced outside for Max's convertible, and saw it parked nearby. That meant they'd taken Darcie's car, and maybe he'd be back extremely late tonight to get his. Or perhaps tomorrow morning. That last thought haunted Ava. Darcie would be texting her tomorrow to give the full report. Ava prayed she would censor the tawdrier details.

She had been kissed once by Max simply so that he could prove a point, and she could only imagine what it might be like to kiss him now that she'd fallen in love. Off-the-charts hot, probably. And she didn't want to think about that happening with another woman. Even Darcie.

Wandering outside, Ava walked along the beach barefoot. It would be okay. She'd weathered bigger disappointments in her life, right? It wasn't as if she already knew what it was like to love and be loved by Max. She'd never find out, so she'd never lose him, and that was for the best. Unfortunately, her stomach didn't seem to agree with this conclusion. It rolled and pitched, tight as a drum.

Removing her red scarf, she let it fly behind her like a kite in the salty breeze.

There were other couples walking along the beach, holding hands, and she sensed, more so than heard, someone behind her. When she turned to offer that someone a ready and practiced smile, it was Max.

Alone.

The smile went south, and her heart gave a powerful thud at seeing him, never mind that he wasn't where he should be. He was here, now, and looked so comfortable in his own skin as he strode toward her with purpose. She gave him a quick assessment. His movements were determined, but they weren't sharp and angry. They were...something else.

"What are you *doing* here?"

"I was invited."

"Where's Darcie? She told me you two were leaving. Going somewhere a little more intimate."

He'd reached her and his body blocked the bright shimmer of the full moon. "Well, we didn't."

Utter indignation swept through her. Not only had he toyed with Darcie's emotions, he'd inadvertently played with Ava's. She'd tortured herself for days with images of Max and Darcie's first incredible meeting. Sparks flying all over kingdom come. Later, their opulent and extravagant wedding day. Their future children, who would look like perfect carbon copies of their gorgeous parents.

She couldn't take this anymore.

"Don't tell me you find fault with her, too. After all I've been through, and how hard I worked to find you someone perfect. I just can't even begin to understand you." Her palms went up. "You must want something that doesn't exist. You—"

And then he reached for her in one smooth and fluid movement, pulled her close and kissed her. His hand was on the nape of her neck, holding her there, and warm lips were moving over hers before she could finish her sentence. Those lips were soft and hard at the same time. His tongue was deep and penetrating.

Her brain froze, her heart stopped, but the rest of her body woke up. Heat pulsed between her thighs, hitting hard and fast as a wave.

He pulled back slightly and smiled against her lips. "Do you *ever* shut up?"

"Max," she breathed, cupping his face. Oh, the stubble on his jaw. Hard bristle and prickly to her touch. "Wh-what's going on here?"

"I want you to do something for me."

"Sorry, but I can't find you anyone better than Darcie. I'm done."

"Yes, you are. I want you to throw away that stupid list I gave you."

"Wh-why?" She tipped her chin to meet his eyes.

"Delete it." He cuffed her wrists. "Please."

"But—"

"Listen. I might be stupid when it comes to love, but I think we have something here. Something real. Am I wrong?"

Her heart pounded hard enough for her to hear it above the surf. "N-no. I'm right there with you."

Then he kissed her again, even though she thought they probably had a few more things to talk about. But oh, well, maybe later. Much later. His hands had lowered to her butt and he squeezed and pressed her tight against him. Her fingers slid up his forearms to those rock-hard biceps, enjoying the feel of the muscles bunching under her touch. Eventually, she didn't know when, her fingers found his thick hair and threaded through. She didn't want this moment to stop.

And oh yes, she'd been right. The kiss? Off-the-charts sizzling hot.

When they finally came up for air, Ava studied his deep brown eyes, so warm and mischievous.

"I've been wanting to do that for a while," he said.

She didn't know this playful side of Max. "You should have said something."

"I was waiting for you."

"For me?" The sweetness of those words sliced through her and her body hummed with pleasure.

Because since when did Max Del Toro wait for *anyone*?

"I was waiting for you to realize that the spontaneous kiss, and that night on the boardwalk, they meant something." He traced her bottom lip with his thumb.

"They meant something to me, too."

"Good. We agree." He crushed her against him, and she rested her head in the crook of his shoulder, a delightful warmth seeping through her. "Can I take you home?"

"Yes."

She heard panting and worried that it could be her. But then she felt a wet coldness on her ankle and when she looked down, they'd been joined by Sub. For a good boy, he had the worst timing. But as if Sub wasn't enough, Cole came right behind him.

"Come here, boy." Looking stunned, he stopped, and Sub bounded up to him. "Uh, yeah. Hi. I'll just…"

"Never mind," Max said, taking Ava's hand. "We're leaving."

This was similar to the original way she'd pictured Max "dating," just taking his woman, and the woman was her!

"I'm supposed to help clean up," Ava said.

"Don't worry about that," Valerie called from a few feet behind Cole, where she'd appeared. "You helped set up."

"Are you sure?" Ava said.

"Thanks," Max said at the same time.

He was definitely better at getting what he wanted.

Valerie smiled knowingly, crossed her arms and nodded. "Cole and I will take care of it. Right, baby?"

"Yeah, get goin', you crazy kids," Cole added, holding Sub's collar to keep him from running back to Max.

Max began to tug her along, and she half expected him to throw her over his shoulder like his spoils after a particularly tough battle.

Then he stopped. "You probably need your shoes."

Ah, yes. Shoes would be good. And also, her purse. "I'll be right back."

She practically flew inside, where a few people were upstairs, throwing out "ooh" and "aah" exclamations over the view. The caterers had wrapped up and gone, and some volunteers were beginning the cleanup process. Ava found her sandals and slipped them on. She'd wedged her purse in a kitchen drawer. Her phone had several missed calls from Darcie and a new text message. Oh man, she hoped Darcie's feelings hadn't been hurt.

Darcie: Grab onto that man and don't let go, or I will personally kick your ass.

Ava quickly texted back:

What happened? I don't understand.

Darcie: You happened, honey. He couldn't take his eyes off you all night long. Thank you for trying anyway. xo

It was just like Darcie to be so cool, and no wonder Ava liked her. Feeling better now, she put her phone away and was ready to fly out the door when Valerie caught her elbow.

"Hey, girl."

"I've got to go."

"Hang on." Valerie smiled. "He won't leave without you."

"I know."

"So, what happened here tonight?"

"I don't really have time for that."

"You have a minute. Cole is talking to Max."

Oh dear. Probably asking him the same thing. But they were two grown consenting adults and what they were about to do was nobody else's business. Frankly, she wasn't all that certain what they were about to do, but she was ready to find out.

"What do you want to talk about?"

"I love Max. You know I do. But…" Valerie crossed her arms. "The list."

"He told me to delete the list. He's done with all that." She smiled triumphantly and shimmied her shoulders. "And I guess Darcie isn't his perfect match, after all."

Valerie pulled Ava into a hug. "I'm happy for you, really. I just want you to be a little careful because it feels like…like you're jumping in."

"I'm sure that's the way it looks, but I've already told you that I have real feelings for him. Now, if you're done here, I have to go before he changes his mind."

"Ha, ha. That's funny. Don't forget, make him work for it." She winked. "You're worth it."

"Okay." If this would get Valerie to let her go, Ava would agree the earth was flat and deal with it later.

A few minutes later, they were on their way in Max's convertible, the night outside cool and calm without a cloud in the sky. This felt similar to the night of her birthday, with a notable exception. Max held her hand the entire time. And she was looking forward to tonight, unlike when she'd faced her family's metaphorical firing squad. Excitement bubbled up, mixed with a dash of fear. It was similar to standing in line for a particularly dangerous amusement park ride. You knew you wanted to go, knew it would be fun, but you were also afraid you might chicken out halfway through.

Max lived in a home within walking distance of the beach. She'd been to his home once with Valerie and Cole. Tonight, she appraised it all in a different light. Max tossed his keys in a bowl by the door and turned on lights as he went. The home was tidy and clean, dark hues the central theme, unlike hers, where every color on the wheel made an appearance. Leather couch. Coffee-colored curtains for which he got points. A small braided rug with every shade of brown on the color wheel. Manly.

She followed him into the kitchen, which was a bit brighter with recessed lighting and a thoroughly modern look.

"Want something to drink?" Max opened the refrigerator door. "I have pop, beer, water."

"Coffee?" Ava said.

He turned to her, quirking a brow. "Do I dare?"

A black percolator sat on the counter, the kind that used paper filters. "Let me."

"You'll be dealing with an inferior bean, I'm afraid." He reached over her into a cabinet and took out a bag of already ground beans. "Sorry."

The brand was actually one of the better ones. "There's hope for you yet."

Max leaned his back against the counter, arms crossed, a look of thinly veiled amusement crinkling his eyes.

The busywork of measuring out the coffee into the filter gave her courage. "Max, what happened tonight? You had to know I would ask."

He studied the kitchen floor. "Nothing happened. You were right. She's perfect."

Definitely not what Ava wanted to hear but at least it was the honest truth. She could always count on Max to give that to her. Zero subterfuge with this man. She loved that about him.

"Did she say something rude? Come on too strong? That doesn't sound like Darcie."

"No. She was great. I like that she does pro bono work. You're right, she has every quality I listed and then some." He met her eyes. "She's perfect. And I think the only thing wrong with her is that she isn't you."

She dropped the scooping spoon.

He gave her an easy slow smile and she melted. Then there was nothing left to do but rush him. She jumped into his arms, and he caught her easily. She buried her face in his warm and beautiful neck and swallowed back tears. She didn't think anyone in the world would compare Ava to Darcie and find *Darcie* the one lacking.

Max chuckled. "I was watching when you got up to dance on the coffee table."

"You saw that? I was trying to make myself feel better."

"About?"

"Knowing I'd just lost any chance because Darcie was so into you and I just couldn't imagine…*this* would happen."

"You need a bigger imagination."

"I've wanted you for a long time. But you scared me a little bit."

"Yeah?"

"All your grumpiness and one-word sentences. I thought you hated me."

"Listen, I can't stare at the sun for long, but that doesn't mean I hate the sun. I actually love the sun."

"Gotcha. And just because you can't stare at the sun for long doesn't mean you don't enjoy the warmth. Of just…being under it."

"Or over it." He smiled again and this time it was decidedly wicked.

"Either way. And I do realize I'm the sun in this metaphor." She slid down the length of his body.

He tipped her chin, his dark eyes gazing into hers, unflinching. "Do you really need that coffee?"

"No."

Then he hauled her up in his arms and carried her into his bedroom, closing the door with his back. She marveled as he placed her on his big bed as carefully as if she'd been made out of glass. He slipped off her sandals.

She took a quick glance, noting his room looked as if a decorator had decided stark and sparse were the way to go. Only one mahogany chest of drawers. A matching sleek bookcase with a few photos and only a couple of books. A few prints decorated the walls, one of the Lone Star State, another of…

Max had started to take off his shirt, one button at a time.

At the utter sensuality of those movements she stood, slowly unzipped her dress and let it fall to the floor to pool at her feet. Thankfully, she wore her matching red bra and panties set even if she hadn't planned on any of this tonight.

She eased the shirt from his shoulders, those incredibly broad shoulders that were also tan and warm to her touch. Nearly hypnotized by his utter male beauty and grace, her fingers trailed down his chest to his abs, earning an incredibly sexy intake of breath out of him. Max squeezed her breast through the bra, his mouth lowering to tug on one nipple through the fabric, leaving it in a damp peak. Then he slowly lowered one strap, and his mouth was on her bare nipple. She trembled at the sensation of his warm tongue on her bare skin.

Then he trailed kisses up the column of her neck and sank his teeth into her earlobe. She moaned.

"You're trembling, baby," he said. "Are you scared?"

Not in the way she'd thought. Now she was afraid he'd take another look at his list one day and realize she didn't have any of the qualities he wanted. Afraid he'd break her heart because she already loved him.

The sound of his husky deep voice near her earlobe and she shook again, this time with heat. "I'm a little…terrified."

"Don't be. I've got you."

"I know you do." Her hands slid down his arms. "What changed your mind about all this?"

"You were right. That's not how love works. I just didn't see this happening until it hit me over the head."

He gently pushed her back on the bed and divested them both of the rest of their clothes. Then they were bare skinned, sliding against each other, moaning, kissing, tasting. He spread her legs and touched and tasted every tender fold.

"Let's go slow," he said, kissing her stomach.

"Maybe next time," she said, writhing. "Max, please. I want you."

He reached for a condom from his nightstand and protected them both. "Whatever you want."

Braced above her, he drew her arms over her head, and threaded her fingers through his. Sweet heat pulsed through her body and she buzzed with desire. She'd never been readier for a man in her life.

"I didn't see you coming," Max said, thrusting inside her, and they both gasped and moaned.

Then there was a lot more moaning, gasping, and neither of them spoke any actual words for a long while.

Chapter Thirteen

Max woke the next morning with a start. He'd been in a heavy and deep fog of sleep, not the norm for him. Usually he struggled to fall asleep and stay that way. But after an incredible night where a cold *anything* was not part of the menu, he suddenly felt ice-cold blocks on his legs. This woke him, and not in his favorite way. He opened one eye and realized the problem. Beautiful, sexy, wild Ava had wrapped herself around him like a taco. She had a leg slung over him, and her feet were freezing.

Rolling to face her, he disengaged from reminders of the Arctic Sea, and considered putting his heavy wool socks on her feet. If he could find them. Not like he'd ever used them in Texas. And how in the world could she have such cold feet when the rest of her body was like an oven? She slept soundly, and he took a moment to study her. A lock of hair had fallen to cover one side of her face, messy, and… adorable. He pushed it off her face, expecting her to wake up. She didn't move.

Okay, so a solid sleeper here. Not a bad thing. He toyed with the idea of waking her again for another round but decided that was selfish of him. She hadn't had much sleep last night, after all. Neither had he. And it had been the best time of his life.

I didn't see you coming.

For someone who prided himself on goals and meticulous planning, Ava had taken him by surprise. She wasn't at all what he'd expected. And maybe he was a jerk for believing this, but yeah, he had wondered if someone so happy all the time might have a character defect. Idiot. Like with so many things in life, she wasn't black or white. Not all good or all bad. Max lived in those gray areas, so he should have known better.

Last night he'd seen her dancing on that table and something inside of him had shifted. She looked like, sounded like and reminded him of home. Love. Comfort and steadfast security. He didn't know how he could have missed the importance of that. In that second, he realized he wouldn't be able to wait for her another minute. She would be his or he would die trying to claim her. Good for him that she'd been on the same page because he'd never been this lucky.

He should wake her up. They could go sailing, to the boardwalk again, somewhere for breakfast maybe. His only solid plans today were to go through the Salty Dog's books, find some money to give the current kitchen staff a well-deserved raise, and check in with Adam. He could do that anytime this weekend.

He pressed his lips to her temple. "Ava."

Nothing.

"Ava," he said louder. "Wake up, baby."

Nothing. Just as he began to wonder if he should check for a pulse, she moaned a little and opened one eye. She jerked then, as if a little confused as to where she was. When he skimmed his hand from her back to her behind, she seemed to remember, and relaxed.

"Mmm," she said, stretching.

"Are you busy today?"

She blinked. "Huh?"

"Busy. Do you have any plans?"

"I...um...wha?"

So, apparently, his extremely talkative, animated girlfriend couldn't talk in complete sentences when she first woke.

"Coffee," she finally said.

Ah. "Be right back."

When he returned several minutes later, she was sitting up in bed, the sheet barely covering those sumptuous rosy-pink nipples. She smiled at him, or the coffee. He wasn't sure which but either way he'd take that soft curve of her lips.

Rubbing her back, he waited for her to resume her natural ability to talk a hundred words a minute. While sipping coffee, she seemed to study the prints on his wall. He saw the room through her eyes. Originally, he'd hired an interior designer because he didn't know anything about decorating nor did he care to take the time to learn. Cole had been fortunate in that the lighthouse he rented had come practically decorated for him, or at least mostly. But Max had purchased a small home three blocks from the beach and had to start from the ground up. Furniture, drapes, appliances. He hadn't wanted to skimp on quality.

He figured the rest of the house could be nondescript, but his bedroom should have said *something* about him. Right now, it said he lived in the great state of Texas, and that black was his favorite color. At least he had his favorite surfboard standing in a corner, reflecting some of who he was and what he loved to do.

"I need some more photos in here. Or something."

On the bookcase the designer had talked him into buying—she was a Marie Kondo enthusiast—he had been permitted three books and two framed photos. One of him, Cole and Adam, out of uniform and at the wedding of one of Max's sisters. Another of his large family at a wedding a few years ago. There were more of them now.

He'd almost laughed when the decorator had asked him, *Are these really* all *family members?*

Sisters, brothers, aunts, uncles, cousins. Yep, all his family. Loud and large.

Ava leaned her head against his shoulder. "Definitely."

"Still with the one-word sentences?"

"Sleepy."

"How long is this going to last?" He chuckled.

She held up a half-finished mug of coffee as her answer.

Later, after they'd finished showering, involving a little making out, they dressed. She only had her dress from last night, making him feel guilty that he hadn't just taken her back to her place. She'd have been more comfortable there.

But at least Ava had reverted back to her usual chatty self, a surprisingly welcome relief.

"Is this Adam? Is this your mother and father? Whose wedding?" She pointed to the photos and asked questions. "Wait. How many sisters do you have again? Any brothers? How many cousins again? Do they come visit a lot? I'd love to meet them."

When he wanted to take her to breakfast, she offered to cook for him.

"Oh jeez, Max, how old are these eggs?" She pulled out a carton and open the lid.

"Do they have an expiration date? They can't be too old, I guess."

"You don't eat at home much, do you?"

"I own a restaurant. What do you think?"

"That makes sense."

"Do you want to go grab a bite there?"

She came into his arms, her head fitting so snuggly under his chin. "I would cook for you, but I don't have much to work with here."

"Okay, then we'll go." He grabbed his keys, and started to lead her to the door, then stopped. "Ava, there's something else you need to do for me."

She looked up at him, a bit uncertainly, her green eyes shimmering. "Okay."

He took her hands in his and adopted his most sincere look. "You're going to have to tell that Colombian farmer he should give up on you."

She burst into laughter. See, he could be funny, too. Sometimes.

Half an hour later, they were seated side by side in a booth at the Salty Dog, and Ava perused the menu like she'd never been here before.

"What do you usually have?" he asked.

"Um, I don't ever have breakfast here."

"Oh, right. Of course, you'll have some coffee." At her blank stare, he grew confused. "I know I'm just getting to know you, but it seems like you can't really have your fill."

"Um…"

"What is it? Tell me." He threaded his fingers through hers.

"I don't want to hurt your feelings." She bit her lower lip.

"You won't."

"I didn't want to say anything but the coffee here…it's really, really bad. Horrible. The only way I can stomach it is with Kahlua but it's a little early in the day for that." She winced.

"Why didn't you say something before?"

"Well, Cole…he's always so happy-go-lucky. How could I tell him that and ruin his day?"

"First, I think you underestimate Cole's resilience. Do you have any suppliers you can recommend?"

She sat up straighter, brightening. "I'll look into it."

He played with the soft hairs on the nape of her neck, somehow unable to stop touching her. "And when you get your coffee company running, you might be able to supply us with what we need."

"I wouldn't want you to do that because we're—"

"Sleeping together? You didn't let me finish. If your beans are reasonably priced, we'll talk."

"Hmm. You can't sacrifice quality."

Just then the waitress arrived to take their orders, a little slow in his opinion. Joanie wasn't their best waitress, a teenager who only worked weekend mornings, their slowest time.

"Hey, Max. Wow, I haven't seen *you* for a while."

Joanie carried the coffee carafe with her, and now that Ava was here, he considered that could be a little too "pancake house" for their brand.

"Coffee?"

Ava covered her cup. Joanie blinked, and poured coffee in Max's cup.

Get up to 4
FREE FABULOUS BOOKS
You Love!

To thank you for being a loyal reader we'd like to send you up to 4 FREE BOOKS, absolutely free.

Just write "YES" on the Loyal Reader Voucher and we'll send you up to 4 Free Books and Free Mystery Gifts, altogether worth over $20, as a way of saying thank you for being a loyal reader.

Try **Harlequin® Special Edition** books featuring comfort and strength in the support of loved ones and enjoying the journey no matter what life throws your way.

Try **Harlequin® Heartwarming™ Larger-Print** books featuring uplifting stories where the bonds of friendship, family and community unite.

Or **TRY BOTH!**

We are so glad you love the books as much as we do and can't wait to send you great new books.

So don't miss out, return your Loyal Reader Voucher Today!

Pam Powers

LOYAL READER
FREE BOOKS VOUCHER

▼ DETACH AND MAIL CARD TODAY! ▼

YES! I Love Reading, please send me up to 4 FREE BOOKS and Free Mystery Gifts from the series I select.

Just write in "YES" on the dotted line below then return this card today and we'll send your free books & gifts asap!

➡ YES ⬅

_ _ _ _

Which do you prefer?

☐ **Harlequin® Special Edition**
235/335 HDL GRGZ

☐ **Harlequin Heartwarming® Larger-Print**
161/361 HDL GRGZ

☐ **BOTH**
235/335 & 161/361
HDL GRHD

FIRST NAME

LAST NAME

ADDRESS

APT.#

CITY

STATE/PROV.

ZIP/POSTAL CODE

EMAIL ☐ Please check this box if you would like to receive newsletters and promotional emails from Harlequin Enterprises ULC and its affiliates. You can unsubscribe anytime.

"I'm going to have the breakfast skillet with the over-easy egg." He turned to Ava. "What do you want?"

"I'll have the coconut macadamia nut banana pancakes," Ava said, and Joanie was about to walk away when she continued, "And a side order of bacon, plus a side of your hash browns."

Joanie went brows up. "Sure. Comin' right up."

"I'm hungry because I didn't eat much dinner last night. I don't mind paying for my order," Ava said.

"You're not paying."

"Fine. It will be my treat next time."

"We can talk about that." It wasn't his habit to let a date pay for anything, but he acknowledged this was a bit retro of him.

"How long has Joanie worked here?"

"Not long. I'm sorry, she's not our best waitress."

"She has a raging crush on you. Haven't you noticed?"

"No, I hadn't, but I'm sixteen *years* older than she is."

"It's kind of adorable that you don't notice how attractive you are to women."

It was? News to him. "Well, I let Cole do all the primping. It's in our contract."

She squeezed his thigh. "You're pretty funny. I had no idea."

He returned the favor, hand on her thigh, going a little higher than he normally would in public. "Don't get used to it."

"Granted, the humor is a little dry, a little snarky. Just like you."

"If you make another martini reference, I'm going to have to spank you."

"Ha." She smirked. "Again, with the *jokes*."

"I think you bring out the funny in me."

There was a beat of silence and then she looked at him, eyes soft and warm. "That's the nicest thing anyone's ever said to me."

Apparently, he'd hit the bull's-eye with that compliment because her gaze went to his lips.

So, he kissed her, slow and deep, because he wasn't one to ignore an invitation.

Chapter Fourteen

Ava considered herself a modern woman and comfortable in her own sexuality. But still, she felt a little squeamish about going to breakfast wearing the same dress and underwear she'd worn last night. She already felt a little self-conscious with the teenage waitress making googly eyes at Max.

"Want to go back to the boardwalk? Or I could take you surfing depending on the current," Max said, glancing at his wristwatch. "I thought we'd spend the day together."

"Of course, I want—"

Then, Ava lost the power of speech because a sophisticated and beautiful woman wearing a dark pantsuit had just entered the Salty Dog, holding her Prada purse, and looking terribly out of place.

"Mom?" Ava squeezed Max's hand.

He squeezed back, then stood. "Good morning, Dr. Long."

"There you two are." She joined them, pulled out a wipe, cleaned the seat, then sat across from them in the booth. "I went looking for you at your house and the kind lady next door—"

"Susannah."

"Yes, that's right, she said she'd missed you today for your regular Saturday-morning coffee ritual. She suggested you might be here, and...here you are."

"Here I am."

"Aren't you two adorable sitting on the same side of the bench? I remember those days with your father. Max, we were both in medical school, and saving every penny. We ordered one plate and shared it. I lost twenty pounds that year. Oh, my," she said to Ava. "Aren't you a little overdressed for breakfast?"

She should talk, with her Prada bag, designer pantsuit, and wipes.

"What are you *doing* here?"

"After we got back to Dallas, I cleared my schedule. I want to see what your fascination is with this small town. Other than the boardwalk, that is, which seems to be the main attraction." She curled her upper lip.

"Where are you staying? The Lookout?" With

only one hotel in Charming, this was no mystery. "Or will you stay in Galveston?"

"I'm staying with you, of course."

All the air seemed sucked out of the room. This was a wholly unexpected turn of events. Mom had never spent more than an evening in Charming, wanting to get out before all the humidity claimed her hair.

"B-but... Mom, I've got such a small place. Two bedrooms, and one of them is so small I use it as a closet."

"I don't mind."

Joanie came by with their plates, giving Mom a not-too-appreciative look when she caught her wiping the table. "Here we go. Skillet platter, pancakes. Let me know if you'd like anything else."

"Good Lord, Ava. Is *that* what you're having for breakfast? What about some oatmeal, a little fruit?"

"We don't serve oatmeal," Max said carefully.

Mom gave him her cocktail party laugh. "Oh, ha, ha, ha. That's all right. Don't worry about me, I've already eaten."

Ava wasn't sure she'd be able to enjoy her meal with her mother the doctor frowning at her addition of the dreaded butter to her pancakes. But she did it anyway, because hers was a practiced tradition of spitting in the face of her physician parents' neuroses. A little bit of butter here and there never hurt anyone.

They ate silently for a few minutes as Mom chatted on and on about her flight from Dallas. Max chewed quietly beside Ava, a huge and unmovable boulder blocking her from the force of Dr. Katherine Long. Ava had always relied on the miles of separation between her parents to ease her guilt.

"This is your place, Max?"

"That's right. Mine and my partner's."

"It's lovely and...rustic."

"You mean quaint," Ava interrupted. "It's *not* rustic. It happens to be a sought-after establishment highly in demand."

"I've often wondered how these places survive the hurricane season."

Max paused, taking a sip of his coffee. "With plenty of preparation. And the seawall is invaluable."

"I'm sure you thought of all that before you invested your life savings into this place," Mom said, looking around, judging it all. Finding it wanting.

"A great deal. And I didn't invest my life savings. I believe in diversification."

Ava's appetite had evaporated, and she picked at her pancakes. Her stomach took a nosedive after being reminded of what a snob her mother could be. And now Max had seen her up close and personal. He was holding his own with Dr. Long, but what could he possibly be thinking? Max was far too cool and collected to ever lose his temper. She'd never seen it happen and Cole told her Max had only lost his temper once.

"Max and I...we had plans for today."

"We can reschedule," Max said, squeezing her hand.

Apparently, he had not received her silent 911 message. *Man down! Save me! Drowning here.*

"Thank you, Max. You're so understanding." Mom smiled. "I would expect nothing less. Ava, why don't we go back to your place and I can unpack?"

"Unpack?"

She waved her hand dismissively. "Just a few things. I left them with the kind lady next door."

"Susannah," Ava reminded her, irritation spreading like a rash. "And we should go. I hate for Susannah to store your luggage like a concierge."

Max stood and offered his hand to Ava's mother. "So good to see you again, Dr. Long."

"I'm sure we'll see each other again soon."

Max walked them both outside into the bright morning. The smell of cotton candy and kettle corn were already thick in the air. And there, parked in a red no-parking zone, was what could only be her mother's BMW sedan rental.

Max didn't give Ava more than a peck on the lips, obviously censoring for her mother.

"I'll call you," Ava said as she climbed into the passenger seat and strapped in.

"What a wonderful man," Mom said as she drove out of the boardwalk. "You're very lucky."

"You don't have to pretend anymore," Ava said. "We're alone. Obviously, you don't like him. You criticized his restaurant."

"I absolutely did not."

"Please, Mom. *Rustic?* That's another word for *dump*."

"Don't be ridiculous. You know that's not what I meant. Max and I are on the same wavelength. I'm sure we both want the same things for you. Success. Happiness. Achievement."

A few minutes later they arrived, and her mother pulled into the carport since Ava's car was not here. She'd forgotten about that. It was still at the lighthouse. Probably for the best, since Mom would expect the BMW.

Mom shut off the ignition and turned to Ava. "Where's your car?"

"Oh, um, in the shop?"

"In the shop? I *hope* you mean the dealership. Your father will have a fit."

"It's… I'm… There's nothing wrong. Just an oil change."

Mom closed the driver's-side door. "I'd certainly like to see you moving out of this older neighborhood. Does Max have a larger home? Room to grow?"

"It's not like we're getting married! We just started dating."

"Three months ago. A few more months and you could be engaged, honey."

Ava gulped. That's right, she was supposed to have been dating Max for longer than one night. Oh boy. "I don't want to rush into anything."

"Well, *he's* thirty-four. I looked him up. And I'm

guessing he'll be wanting to settle down soon and start a family."

Ava thought of The List. She wondered if Max had decided to let the whole idea of marriage go. When he told her to throw away the list, did he mean he'd stopped looking for a wife? Or had he simply meant he was more open to possibilities not dictated so stringently? Because she hadn't asked for details. Far too busy jumping his bones. Come to think of it, they should probably talk about that…at some point.

Ava crossed the shared lawn, Mom following, and knocked on Susannah's door. She opened it, holding Doodle. He did his best job at a ferocious and protective bark. Ava loved the way he tried. So sweet.

"Stop it, Doodle. These are our friends. Missed you this morning, Ava," Susannah said. "I bought a new Danish from the bakery. It's pineapple, your favorite."

"I'm sorry, Susannah. I had something to do." She cleared her throat. "A morning meeting."

"Isn't that the same dress…" Susannah's gaze swept up and down Ava and then as understanding dawned, her eyes widened. "Oh, um, well, here's the luggage."

She moved aside and pointed to no less than four matching designer suitcases in increasing sizes. Ava turned to her mother, jaw gaping, words failing her. It took two trips to get all of Mom's luggage next door.

"You should have kept this in your car rather than

bother Susannah," Ava said, struggling with the last suitcase.

"I didn't know how long I'd be driving around looking for you."

"You could have called or texted me."

"I don't text. I've tried and I can't stand being corrected. If I meant *duck*, I'd type *duck*. Besides, I can't find my phone."

"Again?"

Dr. Long lost her phone daily. Unfortunately, once it had been found in the operating room, a huge embarrassment. She'd gone back to old-fashioned pagers. Her mother was the most intelligent woman Ava had ever known, and about as absentminded as they came.

Mom was now inspecting Ava's home, presumably for any changes from the last time she'd been here. When her eyes caught sight of the gorilla sitting on top of the couch, she blinked.

"It's a long story," Ava said. "Look, I need to change. Just...make yourself at home."

In her bedroom, Ava texted Max:

I'm so sorry about Dr. Long.

Max: Don't worry about it. I'm tough enough to take it.

Ava: I'll escape as soon as I possibly can.

Max: I want to see you.

Ava: Me too.

She added a heart emoticon for good measure because that's how she rolled.

Maybe tomorrow she'd drop by with some of her roasted beans and surprise him with the real stuff. The idea of supplying the Salty Dog with real coffee held incredible appeal. If nothing else, she could stop adding Kahlua to hers.

After washing her face and changing into fresh clothes, Ava felt much better. Her mother was simply checking in, probably a surprise sneak attack to find out whether Ava had been lying about her relationship with Max. Moving from bohemian types to Max, it was no wonder Mom had doubts.

How convenient to no longer be lying. When Ava emerged from the bedroom, Mom had made herself at home. She'd changed from her pantsuit into her dressed-down "I'm home for the day" look. Which meant creased black slacks, matching sling backs and a silk short-sleeved taupe blouse. Always elegant.

"Would you like something to drink? I have bottled water."

"I'm fine, honey."

Ava sat next to her. "Why are you really here? Is something wrong?"

"All right, you could always read me. Your father and I had a small fight. As you know, we never fight."

"I know." It was weird, actually.

Ava believed every couple should fight. Everyone that deeply cared, anyway. Her parents thought it below their intellect to fight. When there was a disagreement on anything they entered into "negotiations." But maybe Ava shouldn't judge. They'd been married thirty-five years, after all.

"What happened? Did negotiations break down?"

"I guess you could say that. But I finally agreed. Your father said I have to let this go and that's final. You're never going to law school or medical school and he detests the idea of small-town politics. He demanded I back off and let you be. That we've lost that battle."

"Really?"

"He said, and I quote, 'Leave her alone, she's perfect.'"

Oh, Daddy. Ava's heart ached sweetly with memories of her father. He hadn't had much time to spend with her but what little he did they'd spent flying kites or kicking a ball around. She should have known he'd come around.

"So, I'm here to find out what I did wrong."

Ava's neck swiveled back. "*Excuse* me?"

"That's right. However long it takes."

"Wh-what about your patients?"

"I haven't taken a real vacation in twenty years. That insufferable partner of mine owes me. I cover for him every time he gets married. Now it's my turn."

"But, Mom, you *hate* Charming. The humidity. The rain. The heat. It's so much worse down here."

"Honey, that's Texas. Besides, you have air-conditioning."

"But—"

"I mean it. Obviously, my example ruined your worldview of a professional woman. And I want to know why. All of your brothers imitated your father's example. You should have followed in *my* footsteps."

"This is ridiculous! You didn't do *anything* wrong. Just because I don't want to deliver babies doesn't mean that you did something wrong. I'm simply my own person."

"I appreciate you not blaming me, honey, but I'm willing to see my mistakes for what they are. And to simply come to an understanding of where, and how, I went wrong."

This was so typical of her mother. She'd made it all about her.

"For what? So you can do better with your *next* daughter?"

"No, so that I can learn and grow. Isn't that what the therapists are always yammering on and on about? This will improve me as a physician, and as a wife, too."

How could Ava argue with self-improvement? She just wished it could happen anywhere else but in her little home.

"Mom, if you and Dad are fighting, I don't think a separation will help."

"We're not *fighting*."

"Well, negotiations. Whatever."

But Ava felt stuck. On the one hand, her mother was finally willing to accept the choices Ava had made. But as always, it came with a caveat.

She took a deep and unsteady breath. "You might as well find out. The BMW is not in the shop."

Chapter Fifteen

The next morning, Ava woke with a start. Outside, a lawn mower had roared to life. Her central air conditioner hummed lazily. Last night, after the tense conversation that ensued with news of the nonexistent BMW, she and Mom had called a truce. Both agreed they wouldn't tell her father. Mom, because that would cause additional problems she didn't want to deal with at the moment. Ava, because she didn't want to hurt her father's feelings.

Next, they'd argued more over sofa versus bed, Ava eventually winning the argument.

But her mother taking the bedroom meant Ava wasn't quite as insulated from the morning wake-up calls. Outside, the neighbor kids were playing basketball, the ball thudding loudly on the concrete driveway. Kicking the covers off, Ava walked slowly to the bedroom to peek in on Mom. She slept, wearing her black eye mask. By all appearances, she slept soundly, meaning she probably also had her earplugs in.

Ava showered and dressed. She made coffee, then quickly straightened up her living room, folding her sheets and stuffing them, and the gorilla, in her hall closet.

Finally, she called Valerie. "Hey, there. Can you and Cole drive my car back to me, please?"

"Hmm, I was wonderin' about you," Valerie cooed. "So, it was one of *those* nights."

"Max would have taken me back to my car, I'm sure, but my mother showed up and wanted to take me home."

"She showed up at Max's house?" Valerie screeched.

"No, no, to the Salty Dog. We were there, having breakfast."

"Of course you were." Valerie had a smile in her voice. "Care to give me any of the details of the night?"

"We just…well, we connected. I really like him. A lot."

Just might love him forever.

"Oh, sweetie, I'm happy for you. And so glad he threw away that silly list. I was about to hit him over the head with it."

"I had to spend the rest of the day with my mother, and I'm determined to see Max today. But I need my car. I want to surprise him."

"Well, Cole and I are on our way to Galveston for the day, so we can stop by on our way out. And fair warning, Max is dog-sitting for us. The guys went surfing this morning and Max took Sub home with him."

By the time Valerie and Cole brought the car back, it was too late for Ava to make a clean getaway. She was writing a note to her mother when she walked into the kitchen.

"Good morning. Do you have plans today?"

"Well, Max and I have been talking about my coffee beans and I've been wanting to give him a sample. I thought I might do that today."

"Don't worry about me. I brought a book."

"I'm sorry. It's just that…this was all so unplanned. And unlike you."

"I know. You're usually the one who goes off half-cocked."

Ava snorted. "Not exactly. Did you know I researched small towns before I moved here?"

"No, I didn't."

And she'd never asked, either, what had brought her to Charming. Probably had simply assumed it had been another whim.

"I'm sorry, Mom, but I have so much going on and I can't take time off for your visit. I have class at the community college in Houston, so I'll be gone a couple of nights a week."

"Carry on as if I'm not even here."

"How about some coffee?" Ava asked.

"Please." Mom settled on the stool near the breakfast bar that separated her kitchen from the living room. "Have you heard from Lucia lately?"

"I got a birthday card from her, of course."

"She never forgets. All of you get a card on your birthdays. Goodness, how I miss her."

Ava had always been proud of the fact that her mother considered Lucia to be her partner in raising her family, and not just the hired help. She doted on her, relied on her, and never felt replaced by her. Mom was too confident of a woman to feel that Lucia could be any threat.

"You hear from her, too, don't you?" Ava asked, pressing the plunger down on the French press.

"Of course. When someone is like a member of your family for over a decade, that connection doesn't just go away. I wish she hadn't moved back. She's invited me to Colombia many times. I'm thinking of going next summer."

"Are you serious? That…that would be wonderful." Ava poured coffee into two mugs. "She would love to have you."

"Your father doesn't like the idea."

"He'd get over it, I'm sure."

Mom snorted, not sounding like herself at all. "He doesn't get over *anything*."

While that sounded bitter, Ava told herself that her parents were a solid couple. No affairs, no separations, even though more than half of their colleagues were on second and third marriages. Over thirty years of marriage. No, they were good. Sure, they'd probably had a minor tiff over Daddy's sudden support for Ava. Her mother would need a little time to get used to Daddy not falling in line, that's all.

Mom had a shower while Ava cooked a healthy breakfast. Oatmeal, nuts, raisins and sliced peaches. The tub of oatmeal was probably from Mom's last visit. Ava wasn't a complete health nut, but she did try. Near lunchtime, Mom announced plans to take a long walk through the heart of Charming and check out all the tiny boutique stores she'd never had a chance to explore.

"Make sure you stop at the new yarn shop, and the Cutesy pet store."

"What on earth am I going to do with yarn and pet supplies? I saw an art gallery on the way in."

"The Artlandish. You'll love that place. Tell Claud I said hello!"

Finally, Ava drove to Max's house, much closer to the ocean. The salty air drifted through her rolled-down windows, a warm breeze whipping her hair.

Carrying her bag, she knocked on the door once. Then twice. She heard Sub bark from inside, a whiny "pet me, please" bark. Was Max in the shower? Otherwise occupied? Well, she could come back. But a moment later, he opened the door.

His dark eyes widened, but if she read him right, the surprise was on the pleasant side. "Hey, there."

"I escaped."

He opened the door to let her in. "I see that."

Ava bent to pet the whiny Sub, who wagged his tail double-time then, satisfied, hopped on the couch for a snooze.

"Don't let me interfere with whatever you're doing. I just wanted to fix you a fantastic cup of coffee. Then you'll see what you've been missing." She dropped her package and hugged his neck.

Max was slightly disheveled. His dark hair was windblown, he hadn't shaved, and he wore board shorts and a tight tee with a…small tear in it, right at the abs. A *rip*? She couldn't believe that Max owned a piece of clothing with an actual rip in it. Obviously, he hadn't expected anyone but Sub this morning.

Boy, sometimes Ava could be clueless. Max had obviously needed some alone time this morning and she'd ruined that for him. She'd been just so excited to see him that she hadn't wanted to wait. And she adored surprises. Then again, not everyone did. This had always been her issue. Trying to bring a little sunshine even when it wasn't needed.

"Oh, Max. I'm sorry. I should have called first. You obviously want to be alone. Well, you and Sub."

Both of his big hands slid down her arms to settle on her waist. "You're not going anywhere."

"But—"

He picked up her bag and walked it into the

kitchen, setting it on the counter. "Thing is, I wasn't sure I wanted you to know this about me just yet. I'd like to think we're still in the honeymoon period."

"Wh-what? What didn't you want me to know?"

He gave her a sheepish look from underneath those long lashes. "I'm kind of a gardener in my spare time."

"And…that's it?" She wanted to collapse on the floor in relief. Max liked to garden. Shocking, yes, but a good shock.

He smirked. "You look surprised."

"What's wrong with gardening?" She went into his arms, and he returned her embrace. She smelled potting soil on him, a wonderful earthy scent. My goodness, she loved this luscious, slightly rumpled Max.

So…human and real.

"Nothing at all even if I'm a little obsessed. It's in my blood. Remember, I grew up in the picking fields of Watsonville. I've always loved growing things."

Maybe he believed the kind of woman he'd been after from his "list" might not be impressed with a gardener. Thank goodness he'd moved on from all that.

"Did you forget I had an affair with a Colombian farmer?"

He rolled his shoulders. "How could I forget *that*?"

"I want to see what you're growing."

He took her hand and led her through open sliding glass doors to a stone-paved terrace. "I'm no Colombian farmer, but let me show you what I've got."

The home didn't have a large backyard, but it appeared that Max had made the most out of every square foot of space. There were four square wooden garden boxes overflowing with green. Luscious strawberries and cherry tomatoes grew in baskets hung from the outdoor trellis. A complex irrigation system seemed to be at the center of it all.

"I'm so impressed."

"Yeah, well, it's a work in progress."

"You could probably grow heirloom seeds here."

"I've considered it."

"Max, this is wonderful."

"I'll finish here later," he said, pulling her to him. "You got away. This is good."

She ruffled his hair. "Go back to the potting and I'll fix you some coffee. Have you had lunch?"

"No, but I'm going to assume you want to ply me with coffee first."

"You're right about that, of course."

"I'm ready to be your taste tester. But I also... I bought some food. I figured I should." He scratched at his beard stubble.

Oh, my. Was she domesticating Max Del Toro? She loved that thought and held on to it. "First, coffee."

In the kitchen, she busied herself with the first of several batches of coffee. She wanted to give him plenty of samples. Strains of arabica and robusta that she'd perfected. It took her several minutes, using the French press, then she poured the samples into the small espresso cups she'd brought with her to present her product. She carried them one by one outside and set them on the glass patio table.

Sub lifted his head from the ground where he'd been napping, no doubt at the wonderful aroma.

"Try this," she said, handing him the first sample.

She watched as he drank, observing his expression. His every eye movement. But if she expected for him to do a "soft-shoe" as he'd joked, that didn't happen now, either. He was still very difficult to read.

He nodded. "Good."

"Isn't it rich and flavorful?"

"Yep."

"How about this one?" She offered and watched him drink. "Because I think it's a little deeper in texture myself."

"Granted, this coffee is far superior to what we serve. But honestly? I can't tell the differences. They're just all...um, rich."

"I understand. Over time, you develop a palate for this sort of thing."

"I believe you." He pulled her into his arms. "Want to fool around?"

Oh, yeah. She did.

Coffee forgotten, Max pulled her back into the house, where he took off his shirt in the living room and then quickly divested her of her jeans and tank top. Twisting and turning and clawing at each other, they eventually made their way to the bedroom where Max once again proved his prowess. A few hours later, they lay wrapped around each other, Ava's head on his shoulder.

Her fingers glided down his pecs to his abs and back again. "I have some bad news."

"Uh-oh. The Colombian farmer isn't going to let you go that easily."

"No!" She laughed.

"No? Because I'll kill him."

Ava propped her chin on his chest. "Max, be serious. My mother is staying with me for a while."

"How long of a while?"

"That's just it. She wouldn't say. As long as it takes."

"As long as what takes?"

Ava sighed. "Until she figures out where she went wrong with me."

"You're not serious." He tugged on a lock of her hair.

"I wish. My poor mom. I almost feel sorry for her. She can't seem to accept that my not following in her footsteps isn't an insult."

"That's an interesting problem to have." Max pulled her closer and kissed her temple. "My father would have had a difficult time accepting it if I *wanted* to follow in his footsteps."

"Yeah?"

"He worked hard when his parents immigrated

to this country. But he was deprived of much of an education because of the traveling they did from one agricultural town to another. He settled us in Watsonville because he always wanted better for me. So did I."

"We had such different upbringings. I don't mean to sound ungrateful. I—"

"It's not ungrateful to want to make your own way even with all the opportunities you were given. You have to live the life you want."

"I hope you know that you don't have to prove yourself to the world anymore. You made it, Max. You're a success and no one can argue with that. It's all you, and your fierce determination. You don't need anyone to—"

"This is about the list, isn't it?"

"Well, it did occur to me that maybe you didn't think you were enough. That you needed someone bright and shiny on your arm to prove that you've arrived."

"You're bright and shiny." He grinned.

"But I'm not the woman on your list."

He groaned. "I feel like that list is going to haunt me long after I'm dead and buried."

But she didn't regret bringing this up. They were sleeping together now and certain things would have to be aired out. "I don't want to be someone you settled for."

He cursed. "Don't ever say that again. I'm *not* settling."

"Aren't you? I mean, the list was over-the-top, but it also makes sense to have some idea in mind of the woman you want to be the mother of your children."

She felt his muscles tense under her touch so she may have hit on a nerve.

"Why? Who did you picture as the father of your children?" He went up on one elbow and turned to face her. "Or did you not get that far?"

"Christian Bale, of course. You know, as Batman. I thought my kids would enjoy that."

"Okay, smart-ass." He rolled on top of her and pinned her there.

She wound her arms around his neck and grinned. "Actually, I always thought he'd be like my father was when I was younger. Affectionate, playful, sort of…larger than life."

And, she admitted to herself, until now Max had only one out of those three qualities. Still, she'd started to fall in love because she'd followed her heart as she always did. Max had opened himself up to her and she'd found that other side of him. His big heart.

"Those aren't many qualities, baby." He nuzzled her neck.

"They're enough. The most important thing I can give my children is loving their father and putting each other first. Everything else will fall into place."

"Sounds like my parents."

"Max. Is this… Are we a fling?" She needed to

hear the answer because she was already falling for him. Hard.

"What? No! Why would you think that?" He stiffened. "Don't answer that. The *list*. I wish I could burn that damn thing in a bonfire."

"That's not why. I mean, I would be okay with this if it was just a fling."

Liar. There went that propensity to want to please everyone. To be their best friend. She wasn't even being honest with *herself* right now.

He quirked a brow and tipped her chin, forcing her to meet his gaze. "That surprises me because I wouldn't be okay with that. I don't do flings anymore. This is just you and me. We're whatever you want us to be. I'll follow your lead."

"Oh, Max. You're not at all who I thought you were."

"And that would be a hired assassin, right?" His eyes smiled. "I can't kill you with one finger, but I think you know I can do a lot of other special things with my finger."

"Wonderful things. I do love that finger of yours."

"Any other questions for me before I ravish you again?"

Chapter Sixteen

Max spent early Monday morning out on the waves with Cole. As usual, Max had arrived first. Dawn broke as Cole pulled into the parking lot moments later.

"Hey, sorry I'm late."

Sub bounded ahead of them as usual, eager as always to reach the water. Max nodded to Cole and waded out first, carrying his board, then going on his stomach to swim out to the swell of the waves. Charming wasn't exactly known for their surfing community, though the numbers had grown in the past year since he and Cole started coming out. At this point, only the diehards were out, trying to catch a wave or two. Max always consulted his nautical wristwatch and gave Cole the full report, often leaving him feeling like a weatherman.

Today the sky was a swirl of blue and gray, the water cooler than normal. The Gulf was usually a bit like a big hot tub. Having been all over the world with the US Navy and his SEAL team, and in every sea and ocean, he preferred the near-arctic temperatures. But he'd made the best of it here and the Gulf had grown on him. At least in the Gulf there was no need for a wet suit.

Max and Cole didn't much indulge in small talk, the way he preferred it. But after about an hour or so surfing, Max had his fill. Besides, more surfers were arriving, crowding them.

"Valerie wants to have a baby," Cole said, carrying his board.

Sub followed along happily, ecstatic to simply be included.

"Whoa. No kidding. You're not even married yet."

"We're going to do that part first, even though she says she doesn't mind walking to the altar already knocked up. She's going to be thirty-one next month, and she says we better get crackin'."

"Such a hardship. Getting your woman pregnant." Max snorted.

Cole grinned. "I'm not complainin' or anything."

"Are you ready?"

Cole was almost two years younger than Max, and two years ago Max was nowhere near ready to settle down.

"To be a father? I thought my father screwed me up for good, but with Valerie, I can't go wrong. She said the best thing I can do for my children is to love their mother. And that's the easiest thing I've ever done."

"I think it's going to be a lot harder than that."

"Yeah, you're probably right. Anyway, we'll figure it out." Cole hauled his board into his truck bed and smiled. "Is it wrong of me not to want her to get pregnant right away?"

"When *getting* her pregnant is going to be so much fun?" Max slapped Cole's back. "Not at all, bro. Not at all."

Next to his vehicle, Max did the surfer change shuffle, underneath a carefully placed towel. A skill Cole had taught Max years ago. Before Cole, Max hadn't been much of a surfer. Though he'd been raised not far from the coast in California, where there was a big surf scene, he'd stuck to swimming. The Monterey Bay was freezing, and he'd learned how to swim there. It wasn't uncommon for him to swim a mile at a time and he'd pushed himself to go farther every time. He'd been the strongest swimmer in the county, which had been a great start to his navy career.

Max normally went home to shower and change, but today he'd brought along his laptop and wanted to work in the office for a few hours before going home to change. Later, he had a Chamber-sponsored networking event with some of the other business owners in town that he made it a point to attend every chance he got.

He and Cole walked down the boardwalk on their way to the bar, Sub following dutifully behind them. The Salty Dog was at the end of the wharf and past the Ferris wheel and storefronts just now opening up. An ice cream shop that served the best waffle cones on the coast was kitty corner to the Ferris wheel. A souvenir gift store next to them sold magnets in the shape of Texas. The Lazy Mazy Kettle Corn storefront on the corner was a favorite with locals.

Sub occasionally barked a greeting to his favorite people, and more to the point, Cole waved at everyone. That was Cole, a friendly person by nature. Max wasn't much of a waver, but more of a nodder. He now nodded a greeting to Karen, manager of The Waterfront, the fine dining seafood restaurant next to them.

Cole stopped to chat, and when it became clear that he would be engaged in conversation regarding Karen's turbulent love life, Max went ahead. There was a reason they'd decided early on in this enterprise that Cole would be the on-site manager. He had the gift of gab.

Max unlocked and unrolled the cage that covered their storefront. Switching lights on inside, he made his way to the office. It hadn't changed much back here since he and Cole saved the Salty Dog from bankruptcy last year by bailing Cole's father out. The plain office was wood paneled, a real throwback look that didn't suit Max. Otherwise, there was just a desk, a couple of chairs and a short leather love seat behind a coffee table. Sub's dog bed and a few chew toys sat in one corner.

First things first. Max opened his laptop and pulled up the spreadsheets he lived by. A P&L report was generated by income and regular expenses. Cole may have wanted to buy the bar to save his father from humiliation, but Max didn't make warm and fuzzy business decisions. He was a numbers man through and through. Numbers didn't lie or tell a person what they wanted to hear. Max went to work trimming expenses, switching accounts and moving money around.

Outside, he heard the staff begin to arrive as people called out greetings, dishes clanged, knives chopped the aroma of coffee percolated. What seemed moments later, he looked up to see that Sub was lying on his dog bed. A cup of coffee sat on the edge of the desk. He checked his watch and noted he'd been at work for three solid hours and lost track of time.

"Hey, buddy. What? You don't even say hi?"

Then he remembered that Cole had taught Sub to sit on his bed while in the office, until he issued a command. Max gave the hand command, and Sub happily rose to meet him for rubs and ear scratches. He went back to his bed when Max pointed to it.

He'd been so engrossed in his work he must not have heard Cole open the door. But the good news was that he'd found the money to give the kitchen staff a well-deserved raise. He'd go ahead and let Cole tell them, because he had more of a need to be the "good guy" than Max did. Cole hired; Max fired.

He also found some wiggle room with their coffee distributor and might just be able to start serving Ava's coffee instead. He couldn't distinguish between their different properties, but he *had* been able to taste the difference between the swill they served here.

His decision had nothing to do with sleeping with Ava. Well, almost nothing. He wouldn't mind being the recipient of her gratitude. Let's just say that. But whenever Max came across quality, he would try to make the numbers work. He just didn't know if Ava was prepared to supply them with all the coffee they needed. She was a one-woman operation.

There was a knock on the office door and Debbie opened it a crack and leaned in. "There's someone here to see you."

He gulped his coffee, now lukewarm, and grimaced at the taste. "I'm not expecting anyone. Who is it?"

"I've never seen him before." She shrugged. "Says you know him."

Before Max could get up, a big, burly figure of a bearded man appeared behind Debbie, startling her. "Don't let him lie to you. He knows me."

Adam.

"Holy shit, dude!" Max was up in two seconds and

grabbed the big guy in a bear hug. "I thought you were going to call me to pick you up at the airport."

"I have an app." He held out his phone and shrugged, then caught a look at Sub. "Hey, you finally got a dog."

"Nah, he belongs to Cole. Submarine, Sub for short."

Max gave the hand command and Sub got up and came over to sniff Adam for all his worth. He wagged his tail like he'd found his new best friend.

Adam bent down and let Sub get acquainted. "Took a walk down the boardwalk. Got a few looks."

And Adam did look a little like a homeless person. His beard was long and unkempt, his clothes disheveled. He looked like he'd just come off a mountain somewhere. Since he'd been working and living in Montana on a goat farm, this probably wasn't far from the truth. He carried a knapsack on his back, which Max would bet carried all of his worldly possessions.

"It's a little warmer in Texas," Max said, taking a look at Adam's battered leather jacket.

"No wonder I'm sweating." He snorted. "Montana is freezing. I was ready for a change."

"Tired of goat farming?"

"It was just a stop."

And there had been plenty of those along the way over the years. Adam was a young widower. After his wife's death and the end of his military service, he'd been aimless. Jobless, much of the time. A hero without direction. Max owed nothing less than his life to this man, so he planned on making Charming, Texas, Adam's last stop.

"Let's talk about my offer."

Normally, Ava attended the monthly town hall meeting where grievances of every type were addressed.

But this afternoon, she had to go home and check on her mother. Since she'd lost her phone and didn't "do" texting, Ava couldn't check in with her during the day. Mom had indulged in some retail therapy on Sunday, buying and shipping several prints back to Dallas. Though Ava was beginning to wonder if something deeper was wrong with her mother, she couldn't discourage her from supporting local Charming artists.

Ava heard the laughter before she'd even gotten out of her car. Through the screened front door next door, she saw her mother sitting at the kitchen table with Susannah.

"I always wanted a family dog, but my insufferable fool of a husband said they carry parasites."

Insufferable fool?

Ava's throat tightened. The bitterness in Mom's voice was unmistakable. She'd *never* called her father a fool. Far from it. She'd always claimed he was the most intelligent man she'd ever met.

"Hello?" Ava said from the other side of the screened door.

"We're right in here," Susannah said from the kitchen. "Come on in."

Ava opened the door and let herself inside. "I'm glad you two are getting along."

"I'm having such a great time with your mother. She's *such* a kick."

Dr. Katherine Long? A kick?

Her mother sat at the kitchen table with Susannah, Doodle the cockapoo in her lap. She looked relaxed, happy and…she wore jeans. *Jeans*. And a… Was that a tie-dyed *T-shirt* from the local boutique? Her hair was in a ponytail. A ponytail!

Ava blinked. *"Mom?"*

"Did you have a good day?" She beamed, ruffling Doodle's fur. "I did a little more shopping and found this incredible boutique."

"What are you wearing? Jeans?"

Her mother stood, setting Doodle down, and showed off the ensemble. "I'd forgotten how jeans tend to accentuate all my best features."

They were tight and…well, disturbing. Even when they'd been on vacation as a family, Mom never wore jeans.

"I think she looks great. Honey, listen, I invited your mother to the Almost Dead Poet Society meeting tonight," Susannah said. "You're welcome too, of course."

"We should go, Ava! Are you busy tonight, maybe with Max?"

Max usually hung out with Cole during the poetry meetings that Valerie always attended. One of the few times Valerie and Cole were apart these days.

"I'm usually busy tonight and can't make it. But I decided to skip the town hall meeting. They don't need me. I…just try to be supportive."

"Perfect. This might be the only time you can attend," Susannah said.

She didn't want to break it to Susannah, but the poetry club was not where she'd prefer to spend her free time. Valerie had given her the 411 on it, and even she wouldn't attend except to support her grandmother.

Their poetry supposedly gave new meaning to the word *amateur*, but if this would get her mother to open up and tell Ava what the *hell* was going on with her, it would be worth it.

Chapter Seventeen

"Thank you for coming," Valerie said as she enveloped Ava in a hug. "Finally, someone my age at these meetings."

"Valerie, meet my mother. Dr. Katherine Long."

"So nice to meet you," Mom said, extending her hand. "Please call me Katherine. Susannah invited me to attend."

For the meeting, Mom had changed into her normal casual attire of slacks and a silky blouse top, giving Ava hope that she hadn't completely lost her mind. Whatever else was going on, she was still *Mom*, unable to leave the house wearing more than two colors.

Both Ava and her mother were introduced to the rest of the senior citizen gang. There were people

Ava mostly knew through her volunteer work at the senior citizen community center in town. Patsy Villanueva was Valerie's grandmother, now recovering nicely from a stroke she'd had a few months ago. Etta May Virgil led the group and was Patsy's neighbor, as were Lois and Roy Finch, the sole man in the group.

There were a few folding chairs arranged to make a circle with the couch. Mom sat next to Susannah.

"The speaker stands in the middle to recite their poem," Valerie said to Ava. "I just sit here and try to be supportive. Be sure to clap when I do. Here, have a cookie. It makes the minutes bearable. And please, please, please don't judge me when you hear my grandmother's poem. I honestly don't know how we could be related."

"I often wondered the same about me and my mother," Ava mused, taking a bite of chocolate chip cookie.

She should have really brought her coffee beans to this meeting and served the group. Maybe if she ever showed up again. She'd already offered to serve her coffee at the senior assisted living center, but too many of them had switched to decaf on doctor's orders.

They began with Mr. Finch, whose beautiful poem was about Texas. When it came to inanimate objects, Mr. Finch threw his voice to make it sound like the truck was talking.

Valerie clapped, and of course so did Ava.

"It's going to be tough to beat that one."

"It always is," Valerie said.

Mrs. Villanueva was next and as Valerie slunk lower and lower in her chair, Ava listened to a sexy poem about how sex hadn't ended at seventy. It was filled with alliteration, which was kind of cool.

"Jeez," Valerie said, covering her face.

"I think that's beautiful."

"You might feel differently if that was your *mother* up there," Valerie said.

Ava didn't think so. She clung to the idea of her parents being in love after all this time. It gave her hope. Though they'd never been particularly demonstrative, they were intensely private people. By the fourth poem, recited by the group's founder, Etta May, extolling the virtues of antibacterial soap, Ava was cringing. Her mother, who attended the ballet and symphony in her spare time, would laugh at these amateur poets. She believed artists *should* be snobs. Were entitled to be snobs. Then again, she'd purchased a tie-dyed tee from the boutique in town, so maybe Mom was changing. In a good way.

People could change in their sixties, right? Sure, they could. Her mother was close to a retirement she and Dad had planned forever. She was simply opening up to new and interesting possibilities, that's all. Opening up to where they'd travel when they retired.

Susannah and Lois concluded the evening, Susannah with a rhyming poem about Doodle, and Lois with a sweet poem about second chances. Afterward there was tea, coffee—fair enough quality—and cookies.

"Thank you for your sweet poem," her mother said to Susannah. "I love how you think Doodle can sometimes read your mind."

They said their goodbyes after a few more minutes, and on the drive home, Mom didn't say a nasty or derisive word about the evening.

"Mom, thanks for being so understanding," Ava said. "I know this isn't for everyone. Valerie cringes at her grandmother's poems. But she misses her late husband and I think they're nice tributes to him. I'm sure you can relate. You and Dad have been in love for so long, after all."

Her mother snorted. "The man in Patsy's poems sounds like a true romantic. Far from your father, who thinks it's *romantic* to schedule sex."

"Mom! *Please!*"

"A little too much information? Well, you asked."

"Are you and Daddy still fighting? Over me? Do you want *me* to talk to him?"

"No, honey, that's sweet. You may as well know now, I'm thinking of divorcing your father."

Ava nearly drove off the road. A car behind her honked.

"Watch where you're going!" Mom chided.

Ava pulled off the road, breathing hard. "Are you…are you kidding me?"

"I'm sorry. I shouldn't have just sprung this on you."

"You think?"

"It was bound to happen."

"Why was it *bound* to happen? This…tell me it's not about me. Tell me you're not divorcing because he's suddenly supporting my choices."

"No. That's not the problem."

"But why? What went wrong? Did he cheat on you?"

Please, God, no! Not her wonderful father.

"Of course not. Your father has far too much integrity for that sort of thing. We both do."

"Then what is it? If you think you've fallen out of love, I hear that can be fixed, too. Maybe a little therapy. I mean, why not?"

"Oh please. Like your father would ever do couples therapy. He's too *busy.*"

"He'll make time when you tell him how desperately you feel!"

"I don't think so. He's still belittling my profession, after all these years."

"What? You're a doctor, just like he is."

"Please, honey. Your father is a cardiac surgeon, i.e. a demigod in our field. The heart is the most important organ in the human body. Everyone believes so. I take care of women and their vaginas."

"Vaginas are important! And so are breasts. You take care of women and that's important."

"Well, tell that to your father. Honestly, it makes me want to shove vaginas in his face every chance I get."

"Mom, please stop!"

"No, I don't mean it that way. People always say if a man is strong, he has a great set of balls on him. But balls are weak. Now, vaginas? They can take far more than a swift kick. Try pushing out a nine-pound three-ounce baby. Then tell me how strong a set of balls are compared to a vagina."

"Oh jeez. If that's all it is, tell him how you feel. You can't tell me that Daddy doesn't respect your work. I know he does. He was so proud of you the year you were asked to speak at the medical convention."

"Yes, well, I've had a great career and I'm proud of myself, so I don't need *him* to be proud of me. But look, I'm ready to retire. Your father and I have planned our retirement for decades, and now he refuses to go along with our plans. He doesn't *want* to retire! And I'll tell you why. It's because he cares more about his own prominence in the medical community that he does about me. I have begged, I have threatened, and he won't budge. He has many good years left in him, he says. So, I'm afraid it's divorce court for us." She took a breath. "That's why I've been shopping so much lately. It's hard to wrap my mind around leaving my thirty-five-year marriage."

Ava fought the desire to clutch her chest. "Is this why you're really here? Have you actually *left* him?"

"No. This is kind of a...trial run, I guess you could say." She looked out the window and her voice grew very still. "And please note, he hasn't called, or filed a missing person's report. I bet he hasn't even noticed I'm gone."

"Both of you are absentminded at times, but I'm sure he's *noticed*."

Still, Ava flashed back to the time she'd been to summer camp for two weeks. When Lucia had picked her up, she'd run inside the house, eager to see her father. And he'd asked where she'd been for the past *two days*.

"Well…if he hasn't noticed yet, he will," Ava said.

"I refuse to enter into negotiations on this matter and that's what he'll want to do. For once, I need him to put me first. Not his patients. I'm able to balance the two just fine, so why can't he?"

"Maybe he…he just needs a little motivation."

"I don't think so." She patted Ava's hand. "Your father never needs motivation. He knows what he wants and goes after it. We just don't want the same things anymore. Maybe we never did. Don't make the mistake of marrying a man who wants different things out of life than you do. Or maybe even on a different timeline. Make sure you and Max are on the same page right from the start. Otherwise, you'll wind up bitter like me."

Ava ruminated on that thought the entire rest of the drive home. She brooded as she set up sheets on the couch. Stewed on it as she and Mom quietly watched TV, no more talking necessary. Mom went to bed early, saying she had a migraine.

Ava picked up her phone, then put it down again. Picked it up and dialed her father.

He answered on the second ring. "This is Dr. Long."

Ava rolled her eyes. Honestly, what good was caller ID if he never bothered to look? "Daddy, it's me."

"Sweetheart, how are you? How's the BMW running?"

Ava swallowed, her throat unbearably tight. "Um, Daddy? Where's Mom?"

"Probably upstairs. I just got in. Want to talk to her? Hang on."

Ava ought to let him sweat. She should let him search every room of the house, call the hospital, page her, text her, then consider calling the police and filing a missing person report.

"What would you say if I told you that she's been with me for two days?"

"I'd say you're joking. That's simply not possible. I just saw her this morning."

"Think about it. Did you actually *see* her?"

There was a long silence on the other end and Ava heard footsteps. She heard her father calling out his wife's name as he presumably walked through the entire house.

"This is outrageous," Daddy said a moment later. "Why would she leave without telling me? And now, she's not even answering my text messages."

"She lost her phone again."

"Why am I not surprised." Daddy groaned. "She's in Charming with you? But why?"

"I think that's something you're going to have to find out for yourself."

Later that night, Ava couldn't sleep. She tossed and turned, wondering if Mom was going through a midlife crisis, or if she was serious about divorce. She'd seen another side of her mother in the past two days. A woman who didn't simply see herself as Dr. Katherine Long. Someone who understood she was more than a doctor. She was a wife, a mother, a grandmother. She was ready to retire from medicine now and enjoy the rest of her life. Since Ava had never known Mom to be anything but goal-oriented in her pursuits, it was a safe bet that she'd get her way.

With or without Daddy.

Giving up on sleep, she dressed in jeans and a T-shirt, pulled on some sandals and went for a drive. It was another quiet and calm evening in Charming as she drove through town and turned onto the curvy road that ran along the coastline. From here, she could see the nonoperational lighthouse where Valerie and Cole lived. There, just outside on that beach, Max had told her to stop looking for his future wife. The thought was a warm thread that wrapped around her heart. She understood that this highly successful man had finally realized he couldn't plan everything. He hadn't planned on her.

This particular lighthouse no longer beamed a

path to lost sailors, or warned of rocky shores, but when someone was home, such as now, the lighting spilled outside through the porthole windows. When Ava had first arrived in Charming, not knowing a single soul, she'd driven along this windy road. Trying to get her bearings and get to know the area. The lighthouse had seemed like a beacon then, reminding her that everyone found their way eventually. Sometimes with a little help.

Right now, she could use a little help. It felt like her world was about to collapse in on itself when the two people most suited to each other in the world were having problems. It just didn't make sense. She consoled herself with the thought that once her father understood how important their retirement was to her mother, he'd relent. But after hearing him on the phone tonight, his irritation clear as they hung up, she wasn't sure what to believe anymore.

She drove all over their small town, wrapping around it twice, and somehow wound up in front of Max's place. No surprise there. He'd been that shiny beacon for her recently. The kind of man she'd never pictured herself with, but now…they fit. Of course, the stupid list was never far from her mind. She wanted to forget it. She'd begun to see that the man behind it, sexy and sexually experienced though he was, had to be somewhat emotionally stunted on some level. Still, she couldn't stop thinking of him.

She checked the time. It was not quite ten o'clock and the lights were on inside. Just in case, she knocked softly on the door. The door opened but this man wasn't Max. *This* man had a bushy beard, wild hair, and wore rumpled and torn clothes. He looked to be homeless, poor guy.

"Can I help you?" he asked from his towering height.

Good. He *sounded* perfectly normal. "Um, is Max here?"

He stood aside. Ava wasn't too sure about this, but she trusted her initial instincts, and stepped inside. This poor man would not harm her. He was just a little dirty, a little dusty, having fallen on hard times.

"I'm Adam Cruz," he said, giving her his hand.

"Hi. Ava Long."

He nodded. "I've heard a lot about you."

"You have?" She was far more pleased with this than she should have been.

Max appeared in the kitchen doorway. "Hey."

"We just met," Adam said with a chuckle. "I think I scared her."

"No, you didn't," Ava protested.

"It's okay. I have that way about me. It's the beard." He scratched through several thick layers of dark scruff. "I think."

"And the wild hair, too," Max added. "Don't worry, he's shaving and cutting off most of his hair before he starts cooking in our kitchen. Meet our new head cook."

"That would be me. Speaking of shaving, I was

about to do that. Please excuse me. It was nice meeting you." With that, he walked down the hallway.

"C'mere." Max flashed her a wicked smile, and only then did she realize she still stood a foot from the front door in the foyer.

Maybe he had scared her a little bit.

"He's very polite." She went into Max's open arms. Those arms were toasty and strong as he held her tightly against him.

She needed this hug tonight. Needed him, and all the strength and warmth that seeped into her.

Max took her hand, led her outside to his small patio and spoke in a hushed tone. "I know it doesn't look that way, and he would never talk about this, but that man you just met is a highly decorated navy SEAL."

"Oh, my goodness. He's fallen on hard times?"

Max nodded. "The transition to becoming a civilian hasn't been easy for him. But Adam surprised me today by coming down from Montana earlier than I thought."

"Is he staying with you?"

Max scowled a little, then shoved a hand through his thick hair. "Yeah. I'm sorry. This is temporary, he'll find his own place soon. Believe me, he'd be camping somewhere tonight if I hadn't insisted. I didn't want Valerie and Cole to put him up, so that left me. Considering I owe this man my life, it's the least I can do for him."

In addition to offering him a job and a brand-new start.

But the thought that Max had been in the position to require saving by anyone was a stark reminder of his past. The men never discussed this. Valerie said Cole didn't talk about that part of his life and the Special Forces team both he and Max had been a part of. She imagined it was the same with Max. Suffice it to say they'd been in some dicey situations all over the globe and lived to tell about it. She knew better than to press for details.

"Aw. You're one of the good guys." She threaded her fingers through his.

He brought their hands up to his lips and brushed a kiss across her knuckles. "Don't tell anyone."

And to think she'd imagined not long ago that this man might not really have a heart. He had a huge one, from the looks of it, even if he hid it well beneath a grumpy exterior. A heart for his friends, a heart for his family, for this community.

And she hoped, a heart for her.

A feeling very close to delight pulsed through her, even if moments ago she'd been near despair. But Max had a way of rearranging her thoughts. Of distracting her. She studied his lips, willing him to kiss her.

He made no move, but his mouth twitched in the start of a smile. "Do it."

"Do what?"

"If you want to kiss me, do it."

She did, smiling, closing the short distance between them and going on tiptoes. Of course, he had to meet her halfway, bending to close the height difference between them. The kiss wasn't sweet. Their kisses never had been. His fingers fisting in her hair, he tugged her closer still, holding her there. She moved over his mouth, initiating the kiss, teasing, but he quickly took over. His mouth plundered hers, taking possession. Staking his claim because she was his.

That's how it felt.

"You do remember that I have an extra bedroom?" he said against her lips. "Adam is staying in the spare room."

And with that, he took her hand and led her back inside the house, and straight to his bedroom.

Chapter Eighteen

The next morning, Ava rolled out of bed before dawn, dressed in the dark and tiptoed out of the bedroom so as not to wake Max. She *hated* her morning look, not to mention her absolute inability to formulate sentences before she'd had coffee. It wasn't cute. That first morning after with Max had been so embarrassing for her, even if he'd been so sweet and patient.

She kissed Max lightly on the cheek, then crept down the hallway in hopes she also wouldn't wake Adam. Besides, she had every intention of getting home before her mother realized she'd even been gone.

"Good morning," said a deep voice from behind her.

She turned, and gasped a little, because Adam

had shaved his beard, *and* his head, and looked like a completely different person. Also, he was some-one who could speak coherently before coffee. This was patently unfair.

"You in some kind of a hurry?"

"Yes. I mean…no." She shook her head. "I didn't mean to wake you. Sorry."

"No worries. I don't get much sleep these days." He shrugged.

She waved goodbye, not trusting any more of this thing called *conversation* before caffeine. At home, she slammed coffee down, showered and changed before her mother even woke.

She'd been at the office bright and early, read-ing and responding to emails, when Max stormed through the door. He hadn't shaved, wore board shorts and a Salty Dog T-shirt. Her reaction to the sight of him felt nearly primal. She wanted to tackle him, but he looked…hostile. His eyes were dark and intense, his jaw tight.

"What's wrong?" She stood and came from be-hind her desk.

"I woke up this morning and you weren't there." He shoved a hand through his hair, and it spiked up adorably. "Was that…last night…a *booty* call?"

"What? No! Why would you think—"

Then she mentally reviewed what she'd done, dropping by late and unexpectedly, leaving early the next morning before he woke. For all he knew she'd left much earlier than she had. She face-palmed. Max was a man unlike any she'd ever met in her life. He didn't want easy, uncomplicated sex, and he didn't want to be anyone's booty call.

Every woman's walking and talking aphrodisiac wanted…more. And of course, she above all women knew that. She'd seen the list.

She reached for his hands and tugged on them. "I'm sorry, baby. I didn't want to wake you, and since I drove around last night without even telling my mother I'd left, I wanted to make sure to be home before she realized I was gone."

"So, you drove around before you wound up at my house? *That* sounds like a booty call."

Oh man, it *did* sound that way.

She palmed his cheek then, the sensation of bristle under the pads of her fingers doing far more primitive things to her body. "No, it wasn't. I'm not the type. Please, please don't be mad."

He took her hand and brought it to his lips for a kiss. "I'm not mad. I just wanted to wake up next to you."

"Oh, Max," she whispered. "You are constantly surprising me."

"This shouldn't surprise you. In case you didn't know by now, I'm in. I'm all in with us. Are you?"

This struck her as such a grown-up conversation, and for the first time Ava realized she'd probably never dated or been with a real *man* before. She'd dated boys who played house with her, and maybe that had been her, too. Dancing around relationships but never being serious enough to fully open up her heart.

"Yes, count me in. I know our lives are complicated right now, but this is you and me. Us."

"That's what I want to hear."

I thought you didn't understand love, but you're pretty damn good at this part.

The words didn't make it to her lips because he hadn't said a thing about love. It hadn't even been a part of his stupid list.

"The reason I took a drive in the first place…" she began. "Last night was rough. My mother…she said she's going to ask my father for a divorce."

Max simply quirked a brow, but then pulled her close and with that one sympathetic move, tears clouded her eyes.

"I'm sorry."

She buried her face in his shoulder. "Then Adam was there, and…and the timing was off to tell you. I didn't want to talk about it. I don't know, maybe they'll work it out. I hope so."

"It must have been a shock. They seem perfect for each other."

"I thought so, too. It's hard to watch. My mom… she's different now. She's fun and carefree. Relaxed for a change. No more snide comments. I think, having worked so hard all her life, she wants to retire and enjoy what's left of it. And my Dad, he doesn't."

"That sounds like something that could be worked out. Compromise."

"Hope so, but you don't know my father. He's so oblivious sometimes. They both tend to be absent-minded, but he's ridiculous. I called him and asked to speak to my mother. Do you know he didn't even realize she was gone? Three *days*, Max. Three days and he hadn't noticed."

"I would notice if you were gone two minutes."

She let that knowledge slide into her, warm and sweet. Her hand pressed to his chest, she felt the beat of his heart. Slow, steady. Strong. "I have class to-night, but I'll come by after."

"Good." He took the hand on his chest and brought it to his lips.

The door to the Chamber offices opened.

Ava turned to the man who'd walked inside. "Hi, I'm Ava! Welcome to Charming! How can I help you?"

With a quick chaste kiss, Max left, letting her get back to work.

After work Ava drove to her business class at the local community college. She drove straight to the satellite office in Houston, about a thirty-minute drive. It had turned out that being a student at twenty-nine was quite different than being one at eighteen. At Princeton, she'd been a good student, knowing no other way to be. Then, the endgame had been her degree. Pleasing her parents. Now the knowledge and skill she'd been acquiring was just for her.

Best of all, community college was the real world. There was Marge, a fiftysomething who ran a beauty salon and wanted to improve her skills and advancement opportunities. Jeff was twenty-five and had never finished his degree. He had a few courses left to complete his AA degree. Suzie was the only eighteen-year-old, and she already worked full-time, so took only night classes. There were others, but not many were interested in starting their own business, or if they were, they weren't admitting it. Then again, Ava had mostly kept quiet about her own plans, too.

When introductions had been made on the first day, she'd told everyone that she wanted to understand more about the ins and outs of business to help support the members of the Chamber of Commerce. And that wasn't a lie, of course.

Tonight, she was early as usual and sat in her front-row seat. Her buddies Marge and Jeff came in shortly afterward, always front and center, too. All three might be called teacher's pet in any other situation and none of them cared. They were here to learn. But privately, they occasionally poked fun at their professor, a former CEO who had found another stream of income teaching accelerated courses at an online university and community college. Rumor was that he'd been quite wealthy at one time, having invested in Apple early on, but lost half in a nasty divorce. The other half he may or may not have lost in subsequent businesses. No one actually knew.

He was fortysomething but looked good for his

age. Still, Ava hadn't yet gotten past the fact that he'd asked her out once. He was obviously a rule breaker but seemed to have recovered well from her rejection.

"Hey, Ava," Marge said. "Traffic okay?"

Ava was the only one who came from Charming.

"Not too bad." Ava pulled out her laptop and set up.

"Maybe we can go for coffee afterward," Jeff said.

"Yeah, maybe."

Marge claimed Jeff had a raging crush on Ava, and now, she elbowed Ava and smirked. Maybe she should mention something about Max soon.

"What's up, kiddos?" Mr. Keith sauntered into the room, a smug smile on his lips. "Tonight, we're going over return on investment, or ROI."

"Oh, good!" Ava said. "It's the most important part of a business."

"It sure is," Mr. Keith said, setting up for a Power-Point presentation. "Listen to Ava, kiddos. She knows the drill."

"Thanks, Mr. Keith." She would never brag but she studied every night.

"In fact, class, did y'all know that we have a bona fide *Princeton* graduate with us?"

Ava turned around to see who else had graduated from Princeton. She'd never told anyone. But no hands were raised. When she looked back to Mr. Keith, his smile was tight as he zeroed in on her.

"That's right, our very own Ava Long." He clapped slowly. "Congratulations. That's an Ivy

League school, of course. Class, only a real *genius* can get into Princeton. I know I didn't get in. Most of us would never even think to apply. The cost itself? *Prohibitive*."

Ava swallowed hard, crossed her arms and slid down her seat. She lowered her head and studied her keyboard. Apparently, Mr. Keith *hadn't* recovered from her rejection. She couldn't imagine what else she'd done to offend him. She'd always been on time and respectful. Always turned in her work on time.

He had no right to judge her. Her professor himself had plenty of opportunities and had done rather well for himself before he screwed it all up, but of course he wouldn't mention that.

Many of the students were now staring. She could feel their gazes on her, feel her skin prickle with heat.

"So, speaking of ROI, and the prohibitive costs of an Ivy League education, let's discuss."

With that, he opened up his presentation where he'd analyzed the costs of a Princeton degree with the salaries of a four-year graduate. Ava's palms were sweaty, and she wondered if anyone would notice if she snuck out of here. The perils of sitting in front. Oh, to have been late today, and been forced to sit in the back!

Mr. Keith continued to click through his slides, analyzing cost of room, board, tuition, books. Ava tried to take notes, but her fingers trembled as she hit the keys. Marge squeezed her arm, then went back to her notes. Ava didn't blame her. Marge wanted to learn ROI. So did Ava.

Through the rest of the class Ava had to sit and take notes on how her parents had wasted hundreds of thousands of dollars on an Ivy League education. Because the only graduates making a good ROI were those that went on to law school and medical school, according to Mr. Keith's analysis. Approximately three-fourths of Princeton graduates went on to those careers, or Wall Street. Ava briefly wondered if Mom hadn't slipped Mr. Keith a few bills for this lecture. Because if guilt was usually only an occasional fly that she couldn't swat away fast enough, now an anvil sat on her chest.

Jeff raised his hand. "But should an education really be viewed as a business model? Isn't education itself its own reward?"

Ava sent him a grateful smile, and Mr. Keith went on to make his point. Not surprisingly, he disagreed. A much more economical, just as functional education could be found elsewhere. Where? Anywhere, according to Mr. Keith.

After class, in the parking lot, Marge and Jeff surrounded Ava by her vehicle.

"You need to report him," Marge said. "This is inexcusable behavior from a teacher."

"He's a bully," Jeff added. "We're all adults but give me a break."

"It's okay, guys. I'm tough enough to take it. He does have a point. My parents paid for my education, and yet here I am at community college studying what I'd wanted to all along."

"I'm with Jeff." Marge elbowed him. "Education is its own reward. That's how I grew up."

"I still think you need to tell the administration," Jeff said. "We have an anti-bully policy and I would imagine it includes teachers."

"Sure, maybe I will."

But Ava would do no such thing.

Her feelings were hurt but she certainly wasn't one to keep a negative situation going on longer than needed. It was over. He'd punished her by humiliating her in front the class and that was the end of it. Before she started the drive back, Ava dialed Susannah. She was one of the few people Ava knew still had a landline. Old-school.

"Would you go next door and remind my mother that I won't be home tonight? I'll be at Max's."

"She's right here," Susannah said. "We're watching the fiancé show that you and Valerie like so much."

"That's great." Good thing that Mom had made a friend.

"Honey, why didn't you tell me about this show?" her mother said, having grabbed the phone. "It's such a find. And I thought I had problems! Kind of puts things in perspective, doesn't it?"

"I know, it's great for that." Ava winced.

She didn't love the idea of comparing her life to

someone who simply had it worse. Not exactly a positive approach.

"I'm going to stay over with Max tonight. I'll see you early in the morning before I have to leave for work."

"Okay, honey. You have fun, be safe and make sure *your* needs are met." With that, she hung up.

Max and Adam had been watching the game when the doorbell chimed. Ava.

He tugged her inside. "Adam and I just finished dinner. Are you hungry?"

"Yeah, let me fix you up," Adam said from the couch. "I'm a great cook."

Ava gave Adam a half-hearted attempt at a smile. "I'm more tired than I am hungry."

She didn't seem her bright and bubbly self and Max wondered if there was something else wrong that he should decipher through the magic of emotional connection. "Are you okay?"

"Yeah, I'm just going to go lie down. I don't feel much like talking. You and Adam go ahead and finish watching the game." With that she went down the hall to his bedroom.

Dear God! Should he call 911? The fire department?

Didn't feel much like *talking*?

Sure enough, Adam was mouthing something to him. Then he quirked a brow. Obviously, having once been married, Adam knew a lot more about reading a woman's mind.

"What?" Max went to Adam, palms up.

"Go talk to her," Adam said.

"Something's wrong, isn't it?"

"Obviously." He spoke as though Max were a third grader. "Go run her a bath or something. You've got that nice sunken tub, why not use it?"

But hell, that sounded like a purely sexual move. Max had wanted to move beyond the physical with a woman, and though he and Ava had off-the-charts chemistry, he hadn't veered from his initial goal. The stats didn't lie. They were going to have to cool it somehow and get to know each other.

Adam stood. "This is over anyway. For you, I'm going to watch the rest of the game at the bar. Don't make me sorry."

Feeling a little silly, Max peeked in on Ava, who was lying on his bed, on her side. He'd apparently interrupted her from staring at the wall.

"Are you sure you're okay?"

"Yeah."

"Do you want a warm bath?"

"A bath?" She went up on one elbow, smiling widely. "Um, sure."

Adam Cruz was a genius.

Five minutes later, Ava was soaking in a hot bath. Her hair was piled on top of her head in some kind of design he would never decipher. The humidity in the bathroom gave her lower lip a plump look. She looked edible. He took a wash towel and ran it down the small of her back. If he didn't ravish her in the next five minutes, he clearly deserved the Medal of Honor.

"I honestly thought this bath idea was a sexual move," Ava said.

"Right? I thought so, too. Then I realized…" He cleared his throat. Or, rather, Adam told him. "Well, it didn't have to be."

"But it still can be." She leaned back, revealing her beautifully rosy-pink nipples. "Is Adam here?"

"No."

And God bless Adam for that.

Max pulled off his shirt with one hand, using the other to take off his pants. The water sloshed and rolled when he pulled her small body between his longer legs. Actually, with his long legs, he barely fit in here. He'd tried to take a bath in here once, and quickly realized he'd somehow bought a house with a sunken tub for no good reason.

But the most beautiful of all reasons had appeared in the form of Ava Long.

"Oh gosh, this is what I needed," she said, leaning her head against his shoulder.

"Hmm," he said, wishing he could take credit for the idea. "Do you want to tell me what you're worried about? Is it your parents? More bad news?"

"No," she said softly. "Something else."

And then she explained what she'd been through tonight, with a professor who'd asked her out once, and now seemed to have an ax to grind. The ROI example he'd discussed on a Princeton education was laughable. Max's emotions segued from righteous anger at the jackass to wanting to take him apart with his bare hands.

But what shocked Max the most was the realization that the professor's attitude had been his too once. He'd believed that only the privileged could afford an Ivy League education and this made every single one of them entitled and spoiled rotten. Drawn with one big, broad brush. He'd had to get his education through the United States government, so yeah, he'd been slightly bitter.

For him, it hadn't been the Princeton class, but Yale. Once, at the Naval Officers Ball, a group of seniors from Yale had attended. When one of them, Donna, had attached herself to Max all night, he hadn't complained. Later, he'd been coming out of the head when he heard one of her friends giggling about "Donna slumming it."

That night, he felt certain that somehow the words *worked in the picking fields* might just be tattooed on his brow. He'd then vowed that no woman would ever consider herself to be slumming while with him. Shortly after that, he'd been recruited to the Navy SEAL team and he hadn't looked back. One accomplishment after the other to prove that he'd pulled himself out of the picking fields. To somehow erase that stamp from his forehead.

"I think you should report the idiot," he said now,

pulling Ava closer, lowering his lips to the curve of her shoulder. "He obviously tried to humiliate you. Unacceptable."

"Should I? I don't want to. That will just give oxygen to the whole thing. I want to forget it."

"Sometimes you can't. Ignoring something just so your life will be less complicated isn't the answer."

"You're so logical."

"Yeah, guess that's one of my strengths."

"And your weakness?"

"Why don't you tell me?"

She turned in his arms to face him, her skin luscious, her eyes shimmering. "Well, it certainly isn't the way you kiss."

He kissed her. And kissed her again. She gave him a look filled with hunger and lust. They wound up doing it in the bathtub.

Much later, she lay sleeping in his arms, her face buried in his neck, her sweet-smelling hair on his shoulder. He felt peaceful. Calm. Max had been in conflicts and rescues all over the world. He'd once been pulled unconscious out of enemy territory and lived to tell the tale, but somehow, he'd never felt this lucky in his life.

Chapter Nineteen

Ava's father still hadn't phoned, and he hadn't shown up in Charming for his wife. If he let Mom go, if he allowed her to leave him without so much as a whimper of protest, Ava might never forgive him. A good marriage was worth fighting for. Their *family* was worth fighting for.

For now, she kept her mother's spirits up. They'd gone shopping at Shoe Fly, for dual mani-pedis at Get Nailed, and spent hours happily lost in Once Upon a Book, the used bookstore in Charming. While Ava was at work, Mom took knitting lessons at Hot Threads, took Doodle for walks and was teaching herself how to cook. But she would have to return to Dallas by the end of the week. She claimed this time had simply been a preview of coming attractions for when she retired next year.

"Even when we went on vacation, every day, every hour, was planned. I've honestly never had this much time to myself. Ever," her mother said. "Honestly, Ava, I truly envy your life."

She almost didn't recognize her mother. They were getting to know each other in a way they never had before. And if Daddy didn't want to know this woman, or at least remember who she'd once been, then he was an idiot. Because Katherine Long was *fun*. She wasn't judgmental and condescending. And for the first time, Ava wondered whose childhood and life philosophy had been adopted in their family. Because it had been her mother who'd hired Nanny Lucia, after all. It had been her mother who brought that slice of life and joy into their home for the sake of her children.

And as it worked out, Ava didn't mind spending afternoons after work with her mother.

But nights? Her nights were for Max. His nights were for her. Dates were a bit harder to arrange since she had Mom for now, and her college course; he had Adam. But they fell into an arrangement. Max had come to expect her every evening, no later than eight. And if she was late, he blew up her phone with text messages.

So, every day after dinner, she'd get her mother settled, arrive to Max's, and spend a little time with both him and Adam watching TV or a movie. She'd do her homework there sometimes and Max helped. Then, she and Max would crawl into bed and spend the entire night together. They were discreet, of course, but Adam still couldn't resist teasing them.

"Max, you might want to check for raccoons in the rafters," Adam said one evening from the couch. "That's the critter that moans, right?"

Ava would blush, and Max would call Adam "hilarious," but it was all in good fun. He was a good guy, hardworking and a great addition to the staff at the Salty Dog. Everyone already loved him, and half the waitresses had crushes on him, especially now that both Cole and Max were taken.

Yes, Max was *taken*. She let that knowledge settle over her daily. It had become obvious to everyone who saw them together and they'd made no effort to hide it.

Far less obvious, but also terrifying, Ava was falling in love. She didn't quite know what to do about that, but it was happening anyway. He was so good, strong, kind, and in her mind deserved everything he'd ever wanted. And more.

On Wednesday morning, she'd just finished attending the Chamber's Business Focus Meeting held monthly at the Community Bank. She'd arranged the group to facilitate the networking between home-based business owners offering services. Sometimes the member who sold life insurance could work with the member selling legal insurance. Or the member who created websites could help a member who needed one.

"Ava, do you have a minute?" Bill, the loan officer, said.

"Of course."

She wondered if he'd want to ask about her business plan. Max still had it, having made some changes that he'd already talked to her about. Considering she'd just learned everything there was to know about ROI, and then some, she'd agreed with them.

Bill walked with her from the glass-walled conference room to his office.

"I wanted to talk to you about your loan."

"Don't worry. I considered what you said about collateral and I'm working on it."

He quirked a brow. "You're in good shape. We took a look at your changes and we're ready to give you a line of credit."

"Wh-what?" Confused, her hands shook, and she pressed them together.

"Max brought it in with the suggested changes and we're good to go. We can get the paperwork set up within thirty days or so." Bill looked ready to burst. "I'm sorry, I should have waited, but I saw you here and I was too excited… I'm so happy for you, honey."

"Oh, thank you. Thanks, Bill. This…it's amazing, right?"

He stood to shake her hand. "You're the lifeblood

of this town and I'm so glad we could make this happen for you."

She floated back to the Chamber offices, a little stunned by the news. So, after all this time, this would happen. Her coffee shop. Thanks to Max and his help. She'd have to thank him *properly* tonight. But she didn't have to wait to thank him because just before lunch, Max showed up.

"Hey, beautiful. Can I take you to lunch?"

"You'll never believe what just happened. Bill told me the loan is approved, thanks to your changes!"

He pinched the bridge of his nose. "I wanted to be the one to tell you about that."

"What's going on?"

"Listen, come with me." He reached for her hand. "I have something to show you."

While that sounded a little ominous, she went with him, and strapped into the passenger seat of his convertible, they drove to the outskirts of town. Max pulled over in front of a small abandoned plant. Tall grass grew in tufts along the sides of the building.

Max reached for her, hand on the nape of her neck, stroking the hairs there. "I'm asking you to use your imagination."

"What is this place?"

Old and weathered signage hung on one of the doors, so worn it couldn't even be clearly read.

"Believe it or not, this used to be an old surfboard manufacturing plant. They closed up years ago to move overseas and this building has been available for lease since then."

"Don't you think it's too far out of town for a coffee shop?"

"Yes, absolutely. Now, here's where I need you to use your imagination." He came around to her side of the car and opened the passenger door. He led her to the front of the plant, and stopped her just in front of it, hands on her shoulders. "As you've told me, you start with the beans, right? A superior product. Right now, you're a one-woman operation, and you couldn't keep up with the demand for coffee at the Salty Dog, much less other places."

"The Salty Dog?"

"Yeah, I wanted to offer you the contract, but I need to know you can produce at least enough for our needs."

"Max..."

"Look. You're going to need an influx of cash, but this building is, as you might imagine, a steal. So, I suggest we start here. Lease some equipment, hire a few seasonal workers, get the roasting plant up and running. You create your brand here, from the bottom up. With quality control and production. And after you're up and running, phase two begins."

"Phase two?"

"Phase one pays for phase two. The coffee shop phase. You can either continue to roast the beans here or move a smaller operation to the storefront. Or maybe a little of both."

They'd talked about this, of course, but her head was spinning because once Max got behind her ideas, everything had come together. Fast. She'd been floundering for years, and now it could all happen. No longer a dream. She hadn't said a word for several long minutes, simply staring at the building, clutching Max's hand.

"Ava? There's still plenty to do. You'll need to create the brand. The name, the packaging, everything. This is just a start. The bank loves the idea because they happen to own this building and would love to put it to good use. Win-win." He waited several long beats. "Say something, baby."

"I… I would have never thought of this. But it's great. Just amazing."

"The building is ugly, I know. But that's just cosmetics. That can all be easily—"

She didn't bother listening to the rest, because she couldn't wait another minute to kiss him. Her lips were on his, hands sunk in his thick wavy hair, simply drinking him in.

When she finally broke the kiss, his eyes were smiling. "I take it you like the idea of phase one."

"I love it."

And I love you, she almost said, but kept the words silent. For now.

Nothing in Max's life had ever gone this smoothly and felt so right. He'd started to understand the concept of love sometimes "just happening." Who would have thought his grumpy self would have fallen for the happiest woman in Charming? Who would have thought she'd be the one for him? He wouldn't have ever considered that the man who planned everything would be a good fit for the woman who planned little. But yet somehow, there it was. He'd fallen in love for possibly the first time in his life. This didn't feel messy or unsustainable at all. It felt real. Peaceful.

The same way his backyard garden did, a place where he'd managed to blend in only the best parts of his childhood memories. All without the hard physical work of picking in the fields. Gardening now reminded him of home, family, and love.

Just like Ava did.

While he'd started out with a list of qualities of the ideal woman for him, he'd now reversed his approach. A total one-eighty. Instead, he could write every single quality that made up the wonder that was Ava Long, and *that* would be his list for the perfect woman. She was beautiful and warm, loving, and completely giving. They laughed together often mostly at themselves, and he found her sense of humor far drier than he would have imagined. He'd already personally witnessed that her bright and bubbly wattage could be dimmed by thoughtlessness. Or—he chuckled—before her first cup of coffee.

And now he'd done something for her that he didn't think anyone else could have done in quite the same way. Because he understood what satisfied his woman, and he wasn't talking about his finger. She loved the very idea of helping others and she'd settled into the business community like a brilliant light that couldn't be squashed. Yeah, *his* woman. His.

It hadn't happened like he'd pictured. Love had punched him with a right hook when his face had been turned the other way. When he'd been looking for someone to have on his arm to prove that he'd arrived, prove he'd pulled himself out of poverty, and would never go back to it again. He didn't need anyone else to prove his worth. He'd proved it to himself.

After a long celebratory lunch, he dropped Ava back at the Chamber office, then arrived to the Salty Dog for his bartending shift. He'd close tonight. Cole wanted the night off to plan a special surprise for Valerie and none of their regulars could fill in. After all, the holidays were approaching. People were making plans, taking time off to leave town and visit family. And, true to form, all of the food barrels were overflowing with canned donations. This holiday would be a great one with his friends. After Christmas, he'd take a little time off to head back to Watsonville and see his family. Maybe even with Ava in tow if she'd be willing to come along. His family would adore her, and she'd fit right in with their abundant love for life.

While he expected a slow afternoon, the lull began to dissipate shortly after five, and he was mixing cocktails and serving up wine and beer. He'd turned to place a mojito on Debbie's tray when he noticed that Dr. Katherine Long had taken a stool.

"Dr. Long," he said, sliding her a cocktail napkin. "Welcome. What can I get for you?"

"Do you have a good chardonnay?" She wrung her hands together.

"We do. Let me get that for you." He poured, his worry growing as he watched Dr. Long.

"Thank you. My little break is at an end and I've got to get back to my medical practice." She held up her wineglass in a mock toast.

"I wish we'd had more time to spend together."

"Me too." She offered him a weak smile. "One thing I won't worry about anymore is my daughter. I haven't seen her this happy since…well, since Lucia lived with us. This town is good for her. *You're* good for her."

"I hope so."

"I know it. Something tells me you'd notice if she was gone. You'd get her back if she left you."

If she left you. Even the thought filled him with uneasiness.

His mind refused to go there. "Sure would. Pretty sure I wouldn't be any good without her anyway."

"She's a lucky woman, my daughter. I wish I was more like her. She left home and found her own way. Terrifying though it must have been, a stranger in a new town, and not knowing a single soul. She's a brave one, my girl."

"I think she's a lot like her mother, actually." Max

found that he meant this in every sense. It wasn't just their passing physical resemblance, the straight blond hair and green eyes. "She's strong like you and *because* of you. With another type of mother, she might not have had the strength of character to choose a different path than yours. You don't give yourself enough credit."

"Thank you, Max." She patted his hand and her eyes grew watery. "I think that's the nicest thing anyone's ever said to me."

Max's attention was taken away by new customers and drink orders, and by the time he came back to Dr. Long, she was gone.

Ava nearly floated home to tell her mother the good news. Her dream would finally happen. She already had tons of ideas in her head about branding. Rather than plastic bags, they'd use one hundred percent recycled paper. She'd been playing around with logos for a while, working with *L*s, thinking of something to honor Nanny Lucia. Of course, she laughed, LL Bean was taken, or that would be a nice homage to both Lucia *and* the Longs. But she'd think of something. This, the creativity, was her wheelhouse. She thrived there and Max was a perfect partner, bringing his analytical mind.

When she arrived home, her mother wasn't there. She'd left Ava a note saying that her little respite was at an end and she'd be headed back home in the morning. Ava was really going to miss her.

Without another thought, she picked up her phone and dialed her father. This had to end.

"Dr. Long speaking."

"Yes, Daddy, I know who it is! Don't you ever look at your caller ID? This is your *daughter*."

"What's wrong? Is it the BMW?"

"No, it's not the BMW. For your information, I sold it."

"You did *what*? That's the best car there is on the market, young lady. Superior German engineering. Are you out of your mind?"

"Maybe I am, but what about you? Have you noticed your wife isn't back yet?"

"I'm not worried. She'll have to be back soon. I checked with Dr. Reynolds. She'll be back in the office this Monday."

"Are you sure she's coming back to you, or just her practice?"

"What's that supposed to mean?"

"It means that my mother isn't just a doctor, she's a woman with plenty of other interests. And I know you have other interests, too, besides golf and dissecting aortas. You're more than a doctor if you'd just get your head out of your...your butt!"

"Ava Elizabeth Long!"

"Well, I'm sorry, I love you, but sometimes you're a dummy. While Mom's been here with me, she's taken knitting lessons, taken my neighbor's dog for walks and taught herself how to cook. She's had so much fun, Daddy. You wouldn't have recognized her." She cleared her throat. "Or maybe you would have."

At least he might have recognized the woman she'd been before children and career took over, and the balancing act took precedence over anything else.

Ava had always thought her father practically walked on water. He was handsome, tall, distinguished. Always the smartest man in the room. But he was positively stupid when it came to love. Her previously perfect father's halo had been tarnished. His wife needed him, and he was too busy with his patients, with his own professional self-worth, to even notice.

"What is going on between your mother and I has nothing to do with you. We'll work this out when she gets back. We always do." With that, he disconnected.

He left Ava to wonder if her mother had always been this unhappy, simply trying to please her husband and do what had always been expected of her. Succeed and impress not just through her own efforts but through those of her children, and grandchildren. It had to be exhausting.

An hour later, Mom waltzed inside, hauling a large print from Artlandish.

"Can you have this shipped for me? I'm leaving tomorrow morning, but I couldn't leave this one behind."

"I think you've personally kept Marjorie in business this month," Ava said, helping prop the large print in a corner.

"I'd been on the fence about this one, because

your father will *hate* it." She went hands on hips. "But after his attitude, I think he deserves this."

"Which print is it?" Ava asked, knowing that Marjorie kept some rather...um, interesting art pieces in her gallery. "Who's the artist?"

Mom peeled the paper back enough for Ava to see. It was a rendering of a woman's anatomy, opening up like a blooming flower. By none other than their local artist, the irrepressible Phoebe Cahill.

"Um, wow, it's um...colorful."

She had to smile as she pictured her father's face when he saw this incredible homage to the vagina.

"Breathtaking. I'm putting it over the fireplace in a place of honor and I don't care what your father says on the subject."

They stood there for a moment admiring. Ava swallowed hard. Now or never. Ever since Mr. Keith's less-than-kind remarks, the matter of Princeton had been on her mind.

"I'm sorry you spent so much money on my education."

"What? Where's this coming from?"

"It was recently brought to my attention that I might have received the same kind of education someplace a bit more economical. But you and Dad probably sent me there because you thought I'd be a doctor like you."

"That's true, but you tried to tell us. We didn't listen."

"All that money. I didn't really think about it."

"I've always felt that education was its own reward. Whether you realize it or not, you learned something there that you couldn't have learned anywhere else. I'm sure of it. And you'll use that knowledge. In ways you can't begin to imagine." Mom pulled her into a sideways hug. "In case I haven't said this lately, I'm so glad to have had a daughter. And I'm especially happy that it's you."

The words were a gift. She'd spent years disappointing her mother while loving her in the only way she could. "I love you, Mom."

"Love you."

They spent the rest of the evening eating one of her mother's early attempts at Tex-Mex cooking, a nachos dish with black beans, yellow cheese and canned vegetables that wasn't half bad. Later, they watched a scary movie and made fun of the people walking into dark and dank basements with nothing but a spatula for protection. They made plans to visit Nanny Lucia in Colombia after her mother's retirement next year. Together this time.

Poor Mom. She would go back to her career and tick off the days until she could be free. That's not what Ava had ever wanted for herself. After Mom had gone to bed, Ava lay a while longer on the couch, thinking of Max. His wonderful mouth. Gorgeous deep brown eyes and wavy dark hair.

The silly man had come up with a list to find his perfect wife. There were some similarities between him and her father, she realized. Both were high achievers who were a little dumb when it came to love. But Max had learned. He'd grown. She pulled out her phone to text him good-night, but instead went to The List. Something had been niggling away in the back of her mind. Some little wisp of an idea she couldn't quite grasp. Max had asked her to delete the list, but she hadn't. In the back of her mind, she wanted to remember. She wanted to be able to tease him years from now when he realized how wrong he'd been.

Between the ages of 30-36
Intelligent
Kind and compassionate
Well educated—at least a bachelor's but more is better here
Even-tempered, not easily excitable
Quiet and introverted
Highly successful in her career and/or business
Brunette
Ready for marriage and children

Now, as she read all of his stringent requirements for the perfect wife all over again, she laughed. She hadn't met his requirements, but thanks in part to him, she'd at least soon be able to add "successful in business." He'd almost made that happen for her. Out of the goodness of his heart, because he loved her, or because he had some preconceived notion of who his woman should be? No, she didn't believe that.

Ava loved Max. Loved him with all her heart and

soul for *who* he was. For who he'd shown her he was. Not a perfect man. But she wondered now if her not-perfect man wasn't still after perfection in a woman. Did he love her too, just as she was, or would he try to mold her into someone else? Someone who would one day fit that list. The thought took hold and spread like a weed.

He hadn't said those three little words to her, after all. But neither had she said them to him. Maybe it was finally time to change that. She'd been some-what afraid to say the words out loud, afraid to give them too much power. Because Max was right in a way. Love, real love, was messy. Complicated. It didn't fit any list. She'd found something she would have never expected from love. Somehow, she was a different person. A better one. More introspective and less carefree but in a good way. Love, pure and simple. Unexpected.

Because she understood what she stood to lose now.

Okay, well, that wasn't a pleasant thought. That particular image needed to go. She didn't want to think about life without Max. Loving Max. Miss-ing being able to wake up next to him curled into his warm, hard body.

And feeling a warm, thick thread of love wind around her hard and fast every time he cracked a smile.

Chapter Twenty

Max was invited over to Ava's for dinner the first night after her mother went home.

He came bearing gifts, a bottle of chardonnay from the bar's collection, which she happily accepted with a kiss.

"Are you all right?" he whispered near the shell of her ear while he stroked the inside of her elbow.

She made a soft sound that was extremely gratifying.

Considering what Ava had been through recently with her mother, he was ready to take her mind off her worries tonight. If *his* mother had suddenly announced she would be divorcing his father, he'd have arranged an intervention. Thrown every counselor and self-help book at the problem. Probably brought in reinforcements. The National Guard, maybe. He'd fix it immediately. Because two people who belonged together, who were as well suited to each other as Dr. Long and Dr. Long seemed to be, should be able to find a compromise. There was too much to lose.

"I'll be okay. I'm hoping for the best, you know? Yeah! They'll work it out, they always do!"

That sounded like the cheerleader he knew and loved, and he relaxed. Nothing to worry about here. The delicious smells of garlic and tomato sauce hung heavy in the air. She took his hand and he followed her into the kitchen.

"Should I be concerned? You're near an open flame."

Considering their last cooking experience together, he had every right to be skittish.

"You're funny." She stirred the simmering red sauce. "No need for you to worry."

"Great. But just in case, where's the fire extinguisher? It should be handy."

"All right, smart-ass. It's under the sink."

He checked. "No, it isn't."

"Oh. Well, it must be in the um, garage?"

"You *do* have one?"

"Of course I do! Okay, let's look for it later. Don't judge me by how I worked in a kitchen with an industrial-size fryer during lunch rush hour. I've managed fine so far, and I've lived here two years. No kitchen fires." She pulled down the colander and drained the pasta. "Now, everything is ready so we can eat."

He helped where he could, but Ava had already set the table with bright colorful bowls and a lined breadbasket. They settled into eating, the scene domestic, and putting him at ease. Ava entertained him with stories about some of their local "color" including the resident who once stopped by the Chamber of Commerce to suggest every business allow a "free" day each month in which everything in their stores would be free. To every single resident in Charming. Ava laughed about it now, but she'd spent some time informing the resident of how bad an idea it would be to get their residents—or the world—accustomed to free stuff all the time. He listened to her jabber away and found that he loved the sound of her voice. She no longer annoyed the hell out of him and now he wondered how he'd ever felt that way.

She gave him more details about the week with her mother, finishing off by showing him the print she'd purchased at the Artlandish gallery, and which she'd asked Ava to ship home. The female anatomy in full bloom.

And yeah, well…he was slightly turned on by that um, flower. "Nice."

He played with the soft hairs on the nape of her neck. She also felt the tension between them, lowering her lashes and smiling up at him.

Yes, you've seen me naked.

Now would be a good time to head to bed.

"Oh! Let's go for a drive."

Okay, so not on the same page there. "Sure. Where do you want to go?"

"Let's drive along the coast, with the top down!"

"Why not."

Admittedly, he'd never taken her for a drive with the top down, even though the weather had been perfect lately. Sunny, mild, light breezes. No red morning skies. Just beautiful blue. Not much rain expected until later this month, he'd checked. Even so, while Ava ran inside for a few things, and just before he rolled down the top, he checked again. Yep, weather good. Time for a little romance.

They drove down the coastal road as the sun began its slide down the horizon. Ava held his hand. He'd pulled out a Cowboys hat and she had one of those silk kerchief things tied around her chin. Dark glasses completed the 1950s movie star look, and she looked for all the world like a cover girl. She took his breath. He'd dated beautiful women in the not-so-distant past, but none like Ava. All those other women knew they were gorgeous and used that currency for everything it was worth. They'd toyed with him, speaking in hushed whispers and sophisticated tones. Underneath, there had been nothing of substance. He'd grown sick of it fast.

He pulled over at a lookout spot and he and Ava settled on the top of the back seats. Pulling her between his legs, they watched the sun slide down.

She nestled into him, her head near his neck, eliciting strong pulls of lust.

The surf kicked up. A seagull squawked.

Romantic.

"I'm so glad we did this," she said lazily in his arms.

"Good timing. The weather is perfect. I checked."

"You did?"

"Ava, it's November in Texas. It could rain."

"Oh, yeah. Not a good idea to go for a drive with the top down, huh?"

"Exactly. Some things have to be planned. Would you have made it through Princeton without some planning?"

"I have planned. That was my life for the first twenty-one years, even if the plans were mostly made *for* me. Now I want to enjoy my life and just take it as it comes."

"Well, you won't be in business for long that way."

She stiffened. "I will plan in business, how's that? But the rest of my life, well, I want to go away on some weekends. Go on bike rides and sailboats. Learn how to cook French cuisine. Get a dog. I've already danced on tables and dated handsome men."

"Huh?"

She turned to him, a ray of moonlight catching in her blond hair, reminding him of the first night he'd kissed her. He'd known even then his world would never be the same again.

"What I mean is, I... I'm falling in love with you."

"That's…that's good."

The warmth of those words hit him unexpectedly. He'd been having some of the same thoughts in recent days. Thoughts that this relationship, this *dating*, wasn't business as usual. That this situation between them was one of those love affairs that took people by surprise. He never thought it would happen to him.

She continued to face him, eyes riveted to his, and it had to be difficult spilling her heart out.

"I love the way you take care of your friends. Your loyalty and friendship. I love that you're not afraid to tell the truth at any time. I love how you're this big bad alpha guy who could have any woman he wants but you want something real."

She went on reciting character details that made it sound as though she were talking about another person. Someone amazing and altruistic. Like…the Pope. She saw him in a way he'd never managed to see himself. Because she hadn't seen every side of him yet. She hadn't seen the part of him that tended to obsess over plans, who pushed hard to be better than anyone else, smarter than anyone else. That man would probably annoy her. He annoyed himself half the time.

"You're making me sound like a saint. I'm no saint, Ava."

"Oh, I know you're not. Believe me." She fixed him with that sultry look of hers that made him want to rip every piece of clothing off her. With his teeth.

"I'm falling for you, too." And this was the truth.

Her eyes were warm, and he knew he'd scored a touchdown. Straight into the end zone, flying over everything and everyone in the way. *What was that, coach? A ball or a meteor?*

"What do you love about me?"

"Well, I love that you're no angel." He chuckled.

"Ah, okay. That's cute." She snuggled into his arms. "And what else?"

A cold sliver of panic slid through him. He had the unnerving feeling that this was where he would ruin this. This was where he'd fail. He didn't have the right words because face it, he didn't watch enough romantic comedies. Right now, he needed *something*, something big like John Cusack holding the old-fashioned boom box over his head.

Words. They would be good.

"You can't think of one thing?"

This was vaguely reminiscent of the night she'd asked him about the last spontaneous thing he'd done. But far more excruciating.

"There has to be *something* besides liking me in bed."

He slid a hand up and down her spine. "Sure, of course there is. You're obviously very intelligent, Ava."

She snorted. "Wow, thanks. *So* romantic. I'm getting hot right now. I might just have to order you to take me right this minute."

Of course, she didn't mean a word of that, and he knew this because he was *also* intelligent.

Irritation pulsed through him. "I don't know what you want from me."

She blinked and he caught a flash of hurt in her green eyes. "Why do you love me?"

This felt like a trick question. He couldn't help but think back to his damn list. Somehow, she would bring that up again. Any minute now. While he silently wished he could burn that list in a big bonfire, he would bring it up first so she couldn't blindside him.

"You know that you weren't what I wanted, not what I'd imagined, but this works."

"I'm not what you wanted." She repeated the words slowly, letting them fall around them like bombs.

"No, what I meant is…" Damn, it was supposed to sound more romantic. He reached and tried again. "You're everything I didn't know that I wanted."

Okay, that seemed better, somehow. Her gaze grew a bit softer, which had to be a good sign, but then…damn it all to hell, it was softer because there were tears in her eyes.

"You don't love me. You don't even *know* me."

"Of course I know you!"

"I don't mean the surface me. You haven't taken the time to get to know who I really am." Her breath hitched. "You haven't been listening."

"Ava, just because I don't have the right words for you, that doesn't mean my feelings aren't real."

"It's not about the right words." She pulled out of his arms. "You know what I think? I think you just wanted to fall in love because it was time. Heart, open. IRA, stocked. Your words. And all of a sudden, there I was, and the timing was right. I graduated from *Princeton*. My parents are doctors. The kiss was hot. And now, you think you can mold me into the woman from your list. Little by little."

"No," he said between gritted teeth. "I *don't* think that."

He wanted to take her shoulders and shake her. She'd been there on the night that he'd been introduced to the so-called perfect woman and he didn't want Debbie/Dana/Darcie whatever. He wanted Ava. He'd wanted this…mess. Chosen this mess. All these uncomfortable and intense emotions that weren't doing either of them any good. They weren't productive. He never lost his cool because there was no point to that. But he felt dangerously close to losing his temper now, and at possibly the worst time.

He looked at her, soft and vulnerable, hurting, and for the life of him he couldn't believe he was losing this…gift…so swiftly. But the truth was that he didn't have anything to give her. He felt tapped out. Worthless. Love should be simpler than this.

"You can't think of *one* thing you love about me."

"It shouldn't be this difficult. You're making this too complicated."

He'd never yelled at her before. He never yelled at *anyone*, famously known for being the last person in the room to lose his temper. Grumpy, sure, but an icicle under pressure. But oh, he yelled now, out of sheer frustration.

"*I'm* making this too complicated? You're practically a genius. How can this be too complicated for you?"

Maybe *complicated* wasn't the right word. *Emotional.* Much better word choice. *Excruciating.* There we go. It felt like there should be blood and guts seeping slowly out of a chest wound. It had been stupid of him to go after love with a list, but he doubted the results would have been this painful. This chaos of emotions had taken over his life. Were now running his life.

This whole idea, falling in love, had been a horrible mistake. He needed out.

"Ava." He dragged a hand through his hair. "I can't do this anymore."

Her head jerked back like he'd slapped her. "Can't or *won't*? You want something easy, don't you? Love isn't easy all the time. I'm challenging you to give me more, to be more, and you can't take it. Can you?"

"That's not true. I don't mind a challenge. Most of my *life* has been a challenge. Maybe now I want easy. Uncomplicated."

"And again, you want something that doesn't exist."

"Yeah. I'm sure you're right about that. I'm sorry, but it's over."

The tears in her eyes spilled now, running down her pink cheeks, and destroying him.

"Take me home."

And just like that, Max ruined the only relationship that had ever mattered to him.

Just when Ava thought life had finally started to make sense, she got sucker punched with a sharp bang and explosion. So, Max loved her, but she was too "complicated." She wanted too much from him, for which she refused to apologize. He apparently both loved and hated her because she'd made chaos out of his utterly controlled world.

The next day, she took time to have a good cry, then pulled herself together and took coffee over to Susannah's.

"I've missed you," she said, shoving Doodle into Ava's arms. "But I know you've been otherwise occupied with that extremely handsome Max Del Toro."

Extremely handsome and emotionally constipated. "We're done."

"Oh, honey, I'm sorry."

Ava cuddled Doodle closer, who seem to know something was wrong. He licked her chin. "I'm okay."

She wasn't, but she would be, given time. It had been an experiment in a way, a risk daring to fall in love with a man who had such preconceived notions. Had she been able to help herself, she might have chosen not to fall this hard. But in many ways he'd made it easy.

"That's the spirit! Plenty of fish in the ocean."

"Sure! Of course!" But Ava didn't feel much like a cheerleader today. For anyone.

Fake it till you make it.

After Susannah invited her over to the next Almost Dead Poet Society meeting, and Ava promised to be there, she went off to the post office to ship Mom's artwork. Fortunately, it was covered, as she wouldn't appreciate the wolfish looks it might draw. Only one man could get away with looking at her that way. Only one man was allowed to give her the sultry, "I want to rip off your clothes right now" look.

Her phone buzzed while she was waiting in line and she answered and said hello to Valerie. "I'm in line at the post office. I'm shipping the vagina print to Mom."

Oops. The woman standing in front of her turned and gave her a censuring look.

"Sorry," Ava whispered to the lady and winced.

"The *what*?" Valerie laughed.

"You heard me. I'm not saying it out loud again."

"What happened between you and Max?"

"Why? What did he say?"

"Nothing, but he came over last night. He and Cole hung out and there were a whole lot of *F* bombs being thrown around. I took a migraine pill and went to bed. I take it you had a fight?"

"We broke up."

Mrs. Judgy Lady turned to her with a smirk, as if to say that of course the woman who bought vagina paintings and shipped them to her sainted mother couldn't have lasting relationships. Suddenly Ava was pissed. Really pissed.

"What? Why did you break up?"

"I can't talk about this right now. I'm next in line and my blossoming vajayjay print is about to be shipped." The woman turned to her, her "former principal of a school for wayward girls" frown firmly in place. "Yes, that's right. It's an artistic rendering of a *vagina*. A lot stronger than a set of balls, and nothing to be afraid of. And my mother is the one who bought it! Want to make something out of it, lady?"

Gosh! She was so tired of being nice all the time. Next time someone got her food order wrong she was sending it back. And she was going to tell Cole in no uncertain terms that the coffee they currently served tasted like it had been strained through lettuce. No more Miss Nice Girl.

Valerie was laughing. "I think I'm growing on you."

"Maybe you are, but also, I'm in a horrible mood."

"It was bound to happen sooner or later."

Next, maybe Ava would get up the nerve to tell Max that he was a chump for dumping her. Because she was the best thing to ever happen to that grump, and someday he'd figure it out for himself.

Chapter Twenty-One

Four days later, Max had grown sick of himself. His was a sad state of affairs. He glanced down at his reading material, and fervently wished for a lobotomy. Or perhaps he should stick pins in his eye sockets. Both would be far less painful.

Every morning he woke to examine his chest, surprised he didn't find a gaping wound there. He'd wanted Ava back two hours after he'd broken up with her. But he just didn't see a way to solve this problem. Worse, if she was right and he couldn't tell her *why* he loved her, maybe he didn't.

But unfortunately, he didn't believe that for a second. His heart told him otherwise. It was just speaking in a foreign language.

"Hey." Adam plopped down on the couch. His eyes widened as he took in the books splayed out on the coffee table. "What the f—"

"I don't want to hear any crap from you. And if you tell *anyone* about what you've seen here today, I'll kill you."

Scattered over the table were self-help books for the lovelorn. This was proof of how far he'd fallen. *Love Languages, Speak Her Language, Tell Her You Love Her in Five Easy Steps, 100 Ways to Love Her.*

"This doesn't make any sense." Adam picked up a book, holding it like toxic waste. "Why, God, why?"

"I have my reasons."

"Dude, what *happened*? You could have had any woman you wanted. I remember how you used to just walk into a room and women would practically arm wrestle with each other just to get near you. Somehow, somewhere, something went terribly wrong."

"Yeah, you could say that." He grunted.

"You never had women problems before."

"Well, this isn't just any woman." He cleared his throat. "This is *the* woman."

Adam would understand. He'd loved a woman once and lost her in the most permanent of ways. His wife, a nurse, had died while working overseas for Doctors Without Borders. That particular memory had kept Max up for the past few nights, wondering how he could simply walk away from Ava. The simple answer was that he could not. He still had a chance to fix this. Unfortunately, everything else was far more complicated.

"It's Ava," Adam said.

"Yes. And I know, I'm an idiot."

"Not at all. But I'm surprised you lost her. She was all googly eyed over you, like most women are."

Max explained everything, earning several brow quirks from Adam. So many that Max felt a pull to shave those bushy eyebrows off.

"You're right," Adam said with a blank stare. "You *are* an idiot."

An hour later, they were both elbow deep in the books, having sworn mutual oaths of silence. Max bent over the book in the same way he'd studied for a midterm. Adam relaxed, the book kind of balancing on his thigh.

A couple of times Adam chuckled. "Yeah, that's right. Mandy always used to do that."

But Max felt as though he were reading a book in a foreign language. All these efforts seemed doable, sure, but they were hardly personal. Intimate. They all seemed forced and he was certain Ava would see through this, too. None of them were him, or his style.

Cole breezed in the door a few minutes later, Sub right behind, wagging his tail.

"Hey, what's up?" He made the classic "hang ten" sign, true surfer boy that he'd always been.

One look at the books and he also dropped an *F* bomb.

"Don't judge," said Max. "I'm learning."

Cole picked up *Love Languages* and gave it a quick perusal. He scowled. "What you need is a romance book."

"I don't have any problem with *that part*." Max smirked.

"Hmm," Adam said, scanning through another book now, and nodding to himself.

"Romance books are about a lot more than great sex, you know," Cole said.

Sub licked Max's hand, and he gave the dog a rub.

Adam finally looked up from his reading. "How do *you* know that?"

"Valerie told me." He shrugged.

Max shut the book. "And where would I find one of those?"

"I could probably get one for you from Valerie's stash easily enough. But there's a problem," Cole said. "I'm still fully in touch with my sanity."

"Spoken like the man who's marrying his first love." Max shook his head with disgust. "You're of no help to me."

"Sorry, but you can't study your way out of this." Cole plopped down beside Adam, who elbowed him in annoyance.

"She wants me to tell her *why* I love her," Max said. "And I've got nothing. She's right. It doesn't make sense to love her. She doesn't meet the requirements on my list. Maybe I'm crazy."

"Wait. What list?" Adam piped up.

"Wait till you hear this," Cole muttered.

Max stood and gestured to the front door. "Enough! If you're not going to help me, get out of my house."

"I can help." Cole spread his arms on the couch and smiled. "But you're *really* not going to like it."

Max grimaced and dragged a hand down his face. "Tell me."

"Well, dude, you're going to have to wing it."

On Wednesday, as she left the office on her way to her business class, Ava saw Max in front of the art gallery, speaking to Twyla Robinson. He stood, hands stuffed in his pockets, quiet as he listened to Twyla drone on and on about something or the other. Her squeaky voice and laugh rang out into the cool afternoon. She, of course, flirted with Max. From here, Ava could practically see Twyla's eyelashes batting like a butterfly's wings. Then she put her hand on Max's chest, and leaned back to toss her wavy, long, *brunette* hair. It took everything in Ava not to run toward her like a MMA fighter and order her to take her hands off her man.

But she didn't. She simply stared, for a moment too long, because Max turned as if he sensed her, and caught her gaze. Ava had to look away from the warm, enticing look he returned. Those were sad, puppy dog eyes, and she swallowed back a sob. She ran to her sedan, clicked the door open and sat herself inside. When her phone buzzed, she pulled it out before she started driving, hoping it was Max.

Hey, it was nice to see you today.

Where are you going off to so fast? Twyla has me trapped.

Why didn't you rescue me? We need to talk.

But nope. It was her mother instead:

Got a new phone. Received the print yesterday, thanks for that. Your father and I have reached a compromise. He wants one extra year to practice medicine before we both retire. I eventually gave in, but I had one big ask in exchange. Can you guess what it was?

The next message was a photo of her and Dad standing in front of the blossoming vagina print over its place of honor above the fireplace mantel. Mom's chin was tilted in triumph and a broad, knowing smile, her hand on Dad's shoulder. Dad's head was cocked, his lips tipped in a smirk, as he held up his thumb in the universal "okay by me" sign. Or the "I give up" sign. Yay, Dad.

Ava typed back:

Love this, and love both of you! xoxo

It was inspiring to see how a couple who belonged together could work things out. But Max was right in one way, even if the knowledge washed over her like day-old stale coffee. Her parents had started off with common goals. When they'd hit a rough patch,

they were far more disposed to work it out. And she'd
known that her father would come through in the
end. He loved his wife, that much was clear.

When Ava turned on her car and looked to back
up, Max and Twyla were nowhere to be seen. Maybe
they'd gone somewhere together, or maybe not. It
was none of her business.

Not anymore.

Ava drove to her business class to forget Max and
focus on something she could accept. Instead of re-
membering the first night that Max had sought her
out on the beach and taken her home, she finally con-
quered a true understanding of return on investment.

The next evening, Ava was deep into her homework. A case study on branding, complemented
nicely by a deep dish of Ben & Jerry's. There was a
knock on her front door.

Max? Maybe he was here. He'd seen her yesterday and maybe he missed her like she missed him.
Some days she honestly believed her heart wouldn't
ever work properly again. It thudded in her chest
sluggishly, like it would never be excited again. Even
after coffee. She couldn't get enthusiastic about anything, not even *Christmas*, which would be here in
a month. The vendors had skipped Thanksgiving
decorations and were already stringing their lights
out in anticipation of a month of fanfare. She could
barely manage a smile.

But now, he was here. Maybe. Her heart beat so

hard she could feel it hammering behind her eyelids. She would forgive him, of course. Give him time to figure this out. He loved her; she was sure. No way would those warm chocolate eyes lie to her.

It's just that he was a dumb guy and couldn't figure out why he loved her. Besides the crazy explosive sex, that is. Couldn't figure out that despite their differences, they were far more alike than they were different. They both loved their families, both valued loyalty and hard work. Both regarded higher education as important.

Opening the door, she found Susannah instead. "Oh, honey, I thought you were coming to the poetry meeting with me tonight."

"That's tonight?"

Susannah's gaze raked over Ava, and her own naturally followed. She had on a pair of black yoga pants and a gray shirt that said "Coffee is my superpower. What's yours?" There was quite a noticeable chocolate stain on her shirt, just below her right breast. Nice.

"Good lord above, what is wrong with you?"

Ava ran her finger over the ice cream blob and licked it clean. "Everything…um, everything else is dirty. Laundry day."

"You've got to come with me. There's no way anyone can be *sad* at an Almost Dead meeting."

"Really? I mean, just the name…"

Not exactly cheerful. Then again, that was pretty

much her modus operandi these days. Might as well go with it.

"You can wear something of mine," Susannah said. "Something colorful and bright. I hardly recognized you."

"No, that's okay. I mean, I can…find something."

She dug through the back of her closet and came out with the black "Audrey Hepburn" dress she wore once a year. Not long ago she'd worn this to her birthday dinner, bringing along a man who had surprised her in every way. Putting it on now made her feel somehow new again. Fresh. And you know what, maybe if she put on the tiara she only wore on her birthday, that might bring some of the perky back.

"Well, that's more like it, Sugarplum," Susannah said when Ava emerged. "The tiara is a lovely touch."

Max wouldn't think so. He'd been shocked that she would leave the house wearing a crown on her head where anyone could see it. The thought almost made her smile. He was almost charmingly grumpy…if there could be such a thing.

"Thank you. It's not *everyone* who appreciates a little whimsy."

Turned out, Ava was far more like her mother than she'd ever realized. Tiaras and blossoming vaginas. All good. They were both powerful women who *chose* the life they wanted.

By the time Ava arrived with Susannah, the senior citizens were already in preperformance mode. They grazed on chocolate cupcakes, snickerdoodle cookies, bread pudding and lemonade, rumored to be spiked.

Ava took a sip and swallowed hard. Maybe spiked lemonade was just the thing tonight. She'd go home slightly tipsy and collapse into bed for a long sleep, no time for more thoughts of Max.

Valerie grabbed Ava in a hug. "You look gorgeous, lady. Where's Bogie? Did you bring him with you?"

Ava snorted. "It's laundry day and I didn't want to wear yoga pants and a Ben & Jerry's–stained T-shirt. Besides, it's pretty obvious that Susannah is worried about me."

"We can't have that." She led Ava to their chairs in the back after loading up with cookies. "Get ready. Tonight, Mr. Finch has got something really special. It turns out that in his latest poem, the state of Texas falls in love with the state of Louisiana. I can't even *begin* to imagine what the voices will sound like."

Except for the fact that Lois was originally from Louisiana, Ava couldn't guess. Love was in the air. Mr. Finch and Lois; Mrs. Villanueva, ever in love with her late husband—sigh—Susannah and… Doodle, Etta May and…well, maybe no one for Etta May.

Same as Ava.

Chapter Twenty-Two

Max worked a bartending shift on Thursday night, giving him a relief from all the mental self-flagellating. Forced to focus his energy on mixing cocktails, not his expertise, he could stop thinking about Ava. For a change.

He poured dry chardonnay for Twyla, sitting on a bar stool in front of him tonight. She'd recently started coming around him far too often. The previous afternoon she'd trapped him on the street as he walked by, peppering him with questions about Cole and Valerie's wedding day. Dropping supersize hints that she, too, was in the market for permanent. For family and children. That she'd heard he was, too.

He'd half listened and then…he'd sensed her. Ava, watching him and Twyla.

She'd stood just outside the door to the Chamber of Commerce and given him a look filled with such longing and pain that he'd been sucker punched. By the time he'd extricated himself from Twyla, walking a few feet away hoping that she wouldn't follow, Ava was gone.

Later, he told himself that was a good thing, because he'd have probably kissed the stuffing out of her and begged her to let him take her home. That wasn't the smartest move. He had to be *smart* about the rest of his life.

"So, Max," Twyla said. "I've got an extra ticket to the Bangles reunion concert next week. Want to go with me?"

That stopped him short. Ava had wanted to go to that concert. He'd told her in no uncertain terms he'd rather be dragged through the desert and left for dead. She'd laughed, kissed him and hadn't asked again. He figured she'd go with Valerie. Now he wondered if she was going at all. And damn, she was cute when she sang every terrible song off-key. To him, it had seemed fitting for the music he could barely tolerate. But the least he could have done was take her to the damn concert. He could have worn earplugs.

"No, thanks. I have plans." He wiped the bar.

"I didn't tell you what day." She pouted.

"Doesn't matter. I'm busy all week."

Fortunately, he had more customers, and Debbie brought over some orders to fill. He got busy mixing mojitos, daiquiris, cosmos, with the occasional shot of tequila or whiskey for the "cowboy" crowd. Eventually Twyla must have lost interest and left, saving him from being downright rude.

One of their regulars came in and wanted a cup of coffee.

"I'm sorry about this." Max winced as he poured. "We're getting better coffee in soon."

The man gave him a puzzled look. "Tastes fine to me."

Dangerously close to lecturing him on the swill he'd just served, Max simply shook his head. "Good to hear. Maybe I'm too picky."

Not everyone had the kind of palate that would distinguish one coffee bean from another. He'd been trying to find a reason that he loved her, but it hit him that there were a dozen little things about Ava that made him love her. They were small things, sure, but effectively, they were bigger than he'd realized. They gave her character, made her lovable and unique. Somehow, he'd fallen for some of her *flaws*. Weird.

And then he reached an epiphany. There was one way he could get Ava back. One way he could show her how much she meant to him. She'd never doubt him again. This was the thing to do. He finally had his answer.

He grabbed a cocktail napkin and a pen and started writing.

By the time Adam waltzed out from the kitchen, apron hanging over his shoulder, Max was on his third napkin.

"How about a cold beer?" Adam took a stool. His shift was at an end.

"Sure," Max said and kept writing.

After a couple of minutes, Adam spoke up. "Today?"

"Yeah, hang on."

"What's that you're writing?" Adam grabbed a napkin and started reading. "Oh, yeah. This is good."

Max grunted. "Are you yanking my chain?"

"No, I mean it. Mandy would have loved this. Hell, all women love this kind of stuff."

"I feel like an idiot, but if this is what it takes to get her back, to really have her be mine, it's probably the easiest thing I've ever done."

"Considering where we've been, I'd have to agree."

Finished, Max stuffed the napkins in his back pocket. "I have a big ask. Man the bar for me, would you? I have something to do and I don't want to wait. Call Cole if you have any questions."

He ran home to change first, because the first night of the rest of his life deserved a suit. When Ava wasn't home, Max texted Valerie.

Where's Ava? I need to talk to her, asap!

Valerie: She's with me at the Almost Dead Poet Society meeting. Why?

He blinked. The...what? Okay, whatever. He had to be there with the almost dead people. Probably a nursing home but what a horrible choice of a name.

Tell me where.

The address she gave was in the senior citizen trailer park where Valerie had lived for a while with her grandmother. He had even more questions then, but no matter. If his woman was there, he needed to be, too. When he arrived, someone opened the door before he even knocked. It was the nice Lois, who came into the Salty Dog often with Roy Finch, one of Max's favorite customers.

"Hey there," she said. "You're here for the meeting?"

"Sure." He worried otherwise she wouldn't let him inside.

"We can always use the support. Artists need an audience, no matter how small, I always say."

"Right. Of course."

He walked into an open, wide living room where many of Charming's old-timers sat. In the center of the room, standing, was Susannah, Ava's next-door neighbor. Her poem, while certainly not Robert Frost material, expounded on her wonderful puppy. And Max loved dogs so he could appreciate the sentiment. Plus, everything rhymed.

He caught sight of Valerie sitting on a folding chair when he was ushered into the room, but no

Ava. Then she strolled into the room, carrying a plastic cup. She wore the same dress she'd worn the night of her birthday dinner, tiara and all, and a kick of tenderness hit him swift and clear. She was absolutely breathtaking, and he was so in love with her.

And Ava was staring at him, her gaze raking over his body.

Coincidentally, he was also wearing the same suit he'd worn the night of the dinner. He told himself this didn't mean anything special, but it sure didn't feel that way.

Etta May stood. "Welcome. Are you here to support, or do you have something to share?"

Well…he hadn't really planned on doing this so publicly, but when in Rome… He moved toward the front of the room.

"Actually, I do have something to share."

At first, Ava thought she'd had a bit too much spiked lemonade. But no, there was Max, standing a few feet in front of her, wearing a suit. It looked like the same one that he'd worn the night of their first date. Their first date had been fake, but everything after that night had been real and raw. Painful, at times, but growing pains usually were.

Etta May waved Max to the center of the room. "Go on, now."

He looked so warm and kissable. She wanted to kiss that gorgeous mouth and lie in his strong arms all night.

"Oh, my lord." Ava grabbed Valerie's elbow. "What is happening? Do you see Max too, or did I drink too much lemonade?"

"I see him all right, but I don't know what he's doing here, either," Valerie said, sounding confused. "Does he have a poem to share?"

Ava doubted that. He wasn't much for sentimentality and even thought the Bangles were over-the-top. Love songs weren't really his vibe. Poems she would imagine even less so.

"This isn't really a poem," Max said. "But I came here tonight looking for someone very special. Because I finally figured a few things out. And I have a new and revised list."

Max pulled out some cocktail napkins that had scribbling on them and Ava's heart pulled in a powerful ache. She thought maybe his hands were shaking a little, this big, strong and powerful man, and a wave of love crushed her hard.

"Max, you don't have to—" Ava said.

"It's okay." He nodded. "See, everyone, the thing is, I'm looking for a wife. Someone who completes me."

"My granddaughter—" Etta May began, but everyone shushed her.

"My list is pretty specific," he said to Etta May. "Not many women can fill it."

"Well, if you're going to be that *picky*..." Etta May said.

"In fact, in my mind, only one woman can. My

wife, the woman I'm looking for—" he glanced down at a napkin "—must not be able to formulate a coherent sentence before her first cup of coffee. Must have blond hair, green eyes, exactly five feet four inches tall. Must treat every day with the enthusiasm of Christmas. Must get extremely excited over a coffee bean. Must be my best friend. Must know how to love. Must always be honest even when it's hard for me to hear. Must have feet that feel like blocks of ice. Must always surprise and challenge me, and finally, must love the Bangles and sing their songs perfectly off-key."

An utter quiet fell over the room.

"That sounds an awful a lot like Ava," Susannah said to Lois. "Does he know this?"

"Ava," he said, looking directly at her. "Do you know anyone who fits this list?"

"Oh, Max," she said, and then she was in his arms, and they were both holding each other tight, crushed against each other. "I love you, I love you, I love you."

"Please tell me that you're five foot four because that one was just an educated guess," he whispered into her hair.

"Close enough, dummy."

She cupped his jaw, this wonderful man that she'd fallen for hard and fast. It certainly hadn't been in her plans to fall for the man she was supposed to fix up with the perfect woman.

"I know I had a lot of specifics, but that was before I fell in love. So, now, my list is in reverse. Because everything you are is exactly what I want. What I need." He tipped her chin to meet his eyes. "I love you, exactly the way you are."

"You guys," Valerie said, blubbering, hanging on to her grandmother. "My best friend! And my fiancé's best friend!"

"Congratulations, you two." Mr. Finch stood, holding up a plastic cup.

"I think we ought to rename our poetry group," Mrs. Villanueva said. "Maybe the Love Connection."

"Everyone who attends our group falls in love, sooner or later," Lois said, flashing Mr. Finch a smile.

"Even if you're not a senior citizen," Susannah said. "Valerie, you fell in love with Cole. Now Ava fell in love with Max. It's spreading like a virus."

"Poetry. It encourages love, heck, maybe even brings it about," Etta May said with authority.

Ava turned in Max's arms to face the small group. "But I think you guys missed something. Max didn't write a poem. It was a list."

"A rose by any other name…" Mr. Finch said, shrugging. "It was a charming list."

Ava turned to look at the man she loved with her whole heart.

"You're right. *This* one was a very charming list indeed."

Epilogue

Thanksgiving Day arrived in a whirlwind of activity. Thanks to Ava, Max had been involved in both the packaging and later personal delivering of canned goods collected by the good people of Charming. For the first time in his life, Max got to be on the other side of this equation. The giving side. The grump in him got a chance to experience firsthand the joy in giving to those less fortunate, seeing grateful smiles as they accepted the gifts.

Hard to be grumpy again after that. All these years he'd deprived himself of the experience when he'd quietly given, never witnessing the results. And if there were small children hiding behind their parents, wishing fervently that they didn't *have* to accept charity, well, he had a feeling someday they'd see it another way.

Maybe they'd see that there were good people in the world who simply wanted to help. And maybe someday they too would be on the other side of the equation. Being the giver instead of the receiver.

Afterward, he and Ava headed over to the Salty Dog, which they'd closed for the day in honor of the holiday. Tonight, they were serving a small group of people. Cole, Valerie, her grandmother and the rest of the Almost Dead Poet Society members. Adam, and Ava's parents, who'd come up for the occasion at Max's invitation. Max wished that his own family could be here, but they'd fill up the entire restaurant. He planned on bringing Ava to meet them at Christmas.

They walked inside to the succulent smells of turkey, pumpkin pie, and fresh baked bread. They'd pulled several tables together to make one long one. In the kitchen creating this amazing dinner were Adam, Lois, Mr. Finch, Valerie and her grandmother, who could be heard shouting orders.

"Heat that gravy on a low flame! And keep whisking. Whisking, whisking. Constantly whisking."

"Mrs. Villanueva, I think I *know* how to make gravy," Adam called back, voice laced with irritation.

"Mom, Dad, hi," Ava said, going into their arms. "Thanks for coming."

"It's our pleasure, sweetie," said her father, his arm around the other Dr. Long. "Maybe tomorrow you can show us your coffee roasting facility."

"It's coming together, but we're still far from opening," Ava said. "There's much to do."

"We'd love to hear about it," her mother said.

Max found it interesting that he'd lied to these people when he'd first met them, and yet that lie had become the truth. He wasn't sure they'd ever tell her parents how they'd originally started out. Besides, if the Doctors Long ever saw his first list, they might castrate him. And he wouldn't blame them. He'd have done the same should that have been his daughter.

He'd have to say one thing was for certain: Falling in love? Definitely the way to go. Oh, hell yeah. Every morning he woke feeling like the luckiest man in the world. He and Ava were going to make this relationship work forever because losing what they had was intolerable. Late one night in bed, she'd brought up something Ava called "negotiations." He'd never heard of anything like that before, but it was kind of cute.

Ava had grabbed a pen and paper. "Okay, I know you want children right away."

"Ava, we really don't have to—"

"Yes, we do. I want you to be happy."

"I am happy." He grinned, lying back, hands splayed behind his neck. A few minutes ago, he'd made them both very happy.

She scribbled something on the paper, biting her lower lip thoughtfully. "Can you give me two years?"

"Two years for what?"

"Before we start having babies."

His jaw dropped. Knowing Ava wasn't even thirty, he'd been prepared to wait it out. More important to have children with the woman he loved than to have them on some exact schedule. Yeah, so he'd learned a few things along the way.

And two years didn't sound like long at all.

"Are you sure?"

"Yes. I want babies too, you know. As long as they're yours."

He squinted. "You want a grumpy little Max?"

"He won't be grumpy if he's my son, too."

"Thank God for that." Max tugged her into his arms. "I love you."

"I love you, too, but we're not done, mister." She went back to her list. "Now, about SAT prep. I refuse to allow it to start in fifth grade."

"That's an easy one to agree on. What about science camp?"

And on they went, covering everything from organized sports to how soon their children would be allowed to date. For someone who didn't like to plan, Ava had done a lot of it with him, far into the future. Then it hit him that she was already compromising, because of him, and he fell in love a little deeper.

"And…marriage?" she asked a little shyly, not looking up from the paper.

"I'd marry you tomorrow," he said. "It's going to have to be up to you."

"Well, there has to be a proposal," she said.

Right.

And that brought him to tonight, and the real reason Dr. Long and Dr. Long had been invited. Ava didn't know that he'd cleared it with them beforehand and asked for her father's permission. A little old-fashioned, yes, but it had earned him some serious points with both Doctors Long. It hadn't surprised him to learn that her parents wanted only the best for their daughter and had simply been concerned to see her struggling. No longer. They believed Max Del Toro was one of the best things that had ever happened to their daughter.

The diamond solitaire had been purchased in a hurry. It had set him back quite a bit, but was worth every penny. The words had been practiced, both alone and with Cole and Adam, who had tips from their own experiences. But, frankly, he would wing it. That had already served him well once.

Adam brought out the turkey on a platter, and the rest of the crew followed with the pies, bread rolls, stuffing, potatoes—enough food to feed a small village. Everyone took their seats, Sub lying under the table to catch scraps, and Adam began to carve.

"Who will say grace?" Mrs. Villanueva asked.

"I'd be happy to do it." Mr. Finch stood.

Max cleared his throat. "Actually, may I?"

"Of course, son," Mr. Finch said sitting back down.

Max stood behind Ava, and she turned in her seat and beamed.

"I have so much to be grateful for this year, as I'm sure we all do. Family, friends, a great town."

"Football," Adam said.

"Surfing," Cole added among the chuckles.

"There's one thing I'm grateful for beyond all others, though." With that, he offered Ava his hand and pulled her out of her seat.

A slow murmur rose, then the room became quiet. Sub, somehow sensing something important was about to happen, moved from under the table and sat at attention near Max's feet.

"It's this woman. The love of my life. She waited for a grumpy, set-in-his-ways man to come around."

Now the room was quiet except for the sniffles coming from Valerie and Ava's mother. And also… Ava's breathing. It was slow and measured, steady, her eyes wide, her chest rising and falling as she met his gaze and squeezed his hand.

"Well, she didn't have to wait that long," Etta May said. "How long have you two been datin'? Two minutes?"

Laughter from the small crowd. He hadn't stopped to think that this might be a class participation proposal. But actually, he was relieved. He hated making anyone cry, and Valerie and Ava's mother were beginning to ramp it up.

"Thanks for the comic relief." He winked at Etta May. "But it's been the best two minutes of my life and yeah, sometimes…well, you just know."

With that he went on bended knee, took out the ring from his pocket and slipped it on her finger.

"I promise to always make sure that you're number one, on any list." He winked again, so that only Ava could see. "For the rest of my life. Would you please marry me?"

Sub panted and whined, apparently worried Ava might say no.

"Yes, silly. Of course, I'll marry you!" Ava tugged him up and then they were in each other's arms. He held on tight, determined never to let go of her again.

Around them, everyone clapped, and Sub barked his approval.

"Lucky me." And then he kissed her and started the rest of his life.

The best part.

* * * * *

For more opposites-attract romances, try these great books:

The Lights on Knockbridge Lane
by Roan Parrish

In the Key of Family
by Makenna Lee

Merry Christmas, Baby
by Teri Wilson

Available now wherever Harlequin Special Edition books and ebooks are sold!

#2887 A SOLDIER'S DARE
The Fortunes of Texas: The Wedding Gift • by Jo McNally
When Jack Radcliffe dares Belle Fortune to kiss him at the Hotel Fortune's Valentine's Ball, he thinks he's just having fun. She's interested in someone else. But from the moment their lips touch, the ex-military man is in trouble. The woman he shouldn't want challenges him to confront his painful past—and face his future head-on...

#2888 HER WYOMING VALENTINE WISH
Return to the Double C • by Allison Leigh
When Delia Templeton is tapped to run her wealthy grandmother's new charitable foundation, she finds herself dealing with Mac Jeffries, the stranger who gave her a bracing New Year's kiss. Working together gives Delia and Mac ample opportunity to butt heads...and revisit that first kiss as Valentine's Day fast approaches...

#2889 STARLIGHT AND THE SINGLE DAD
Welcome to Starlight • by Michelle Major
Relocating to the Cascade Mountains is the first step in Tessa Reynolds's plan to reinvent herself. Former military pilot Carson Campbell sees the bold and beautiful redhead only wreaking havoc with his own plan to be the father his young daughter needs. As her feelings for Carson deepen, Tessa finally knows who she wants to be—the woman who walks off with Carson's heart...

#2890 THE SHOE DIARIES
The Friendship Chronicles • by Darby Baham
From the outside, Reagan "Rae" Doucet has it all: a coveted career in Washington, DC, a tight circle of friends and a shoe closet to die for. When one of her crew falls ill, however, Rae is done playing it safe. The talented but unfulfilled writer makes a "risk list" to revamp her life. But forgiving her ex, Jake Saunders, might be one risk too many...

#2891 THE FIVE-DAY REUNION
Once Upon a Wedding • by Mona Shroff
Law student Anita Virani hasn't seen her ex-husband since the divorce. Now she's agreed to pretend she's still married to Nikhil until his sister's wedding celebrations are over—because her former mother-in-law neglected to tell her family of their split!

#2892 THE MARINE'S RELUCTANT RETURN
The Stirling Ranch • by Sabrina York
She'd been the girl he'd always loved—until she married his best friend. Now Crystal Stoker was a widowed single mom and Luke Stirling was trying his best to avoid her. That was proving impossible in their small town. The injured marine was just looking for a little peace and quiet, not expecting any second chances, especially ones he didn't dare accept.

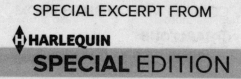
"I won! I won!"

"That you did," he said, laughing and trying to climb out of his own tube. With his long legs, he was having a hard time getting out on his own, so I reached out my hand to help him up. As soon as he grabbed me, we both went soaring, feet away from the slides. I was amazed neither of us fell onto the ground, but I think just when we were about to, he caught me midair and steadied us.

"Okay, so a deal is a deal. Truth. Do you like me?"

"I can't believe you wasted your truth on something you already know."

"Maybe a girl needs to hear it sometimes."

"Reagan Doucet, I will tell you all day long how much I like you," he said, bending down again so he could stare directly into my eyes. "But you have to believe me when I do. No more of that 'c'mon, Jake' stuff. You either believe me or you don't."

"Deal," I said, grabbing hold of the loops on the waist of his pants to bring him even closer to me. "You got it."

"Mmm, no. I've got you," he whispered, bringing his lips centimeters away from mine but refusing to kiss me. Instead, he stood there, making me wait, and then flicked out his tongue with a grin, barely scraping the skin on my lips. It was clear Jake wanted me to want him. Better yet, crave him. And while I could also tell this was him putting on his charm armor again, I didn't care. I was in shoe, Christmas lights and sexy guy heaven, and for once I was determined to enjoy it. Not much could top that.

"Now, let's go find these pandas."

I reached out my hand, and he took it as we went skipping to the next exhibit.

Don't miss The Shoe Diaries *by Darby Baham,*
available February 2022 wherever
Harlequin Special Edition books and ebooks are sold.

Harlequin.com